RIO GRANDE BLACK MAGIC

Hardcover ISBN: 978-1-932113-64-8
Paperback ISBN: 978-0-9657302-7-3
Copyright 2020
Published by Lauric Press
In Conjunction with Wolfpack Publishing

I WANT YOU
GRINGO !
fight in the
MEXICAN REVOLUTION
and be proud to ride with
PANCHO VILLA
NEAREST RECRUITING STATION

Other Titles by W. Hock Hochheim

Fightin' Words
Dead Right There
Don't Even Think About It!
Blood Rust: Death of the China Doll
My Gun is My Passport
Last of the Gunmen
American Medieval
The China Alamo
Be Bad Now
Impact Weapon Combatives
Knife Combatives
Training Mission Series One through Five
The Great Escapes of Pancho Villa

ATENCIÓN GRINGO
For GOLD & GLORY
Come South of the Border and
Ride
With PANCHO VILLA
El Liberator of Mexico!
WEEKLY PAYMENTS IN GOLD TO
DYNAMITERS, MACHINE GUNNERS & RAILROADERS
Enlistments Taken In Juarez, Mexico
* January 1915 *
VIVA VILLA! VIVA Revolución!

TABLE OF CONTENTS

Hock at author's night, Kings School, England

Author's Prologue

After the era of the gunfighter in the 1890s and just before the time of the *noir* detective of the 1920s, a certain kind of "investigator" solved people's problems. German immigrant Johann Gunther was such a person. Army war vet, West Point graduate, former lawman in Paris, Texas, Gunther formed the *Remedies Detective Agency* in Fort Worth, Texas.

Rio Grande Black Magic is the third in the series of the 1900s adventures of Johann Gunther and his Filipino sidekick/partner Jefe.

Anyone can start the series right here with book three. But, it helps a bit to have read the first international epic in the series, *My Gun is My Passport* which places the ethos and ethics of our Western hero in the crimes and wars of foreign lands like India and Afghanistan.

Last of the Gunmen, the second story puts Gunther and Jefe back home in Fort Worth, Texas solving a series of murders, corruptions and crimes committed by the first motorcycle gang that also travels as a minor league baseball team. Sports writer Bat Masterson makes an important appearance in that book. Both the good guys and the bad guys inadvertently find themselves in an international money scheme that leads to a showdown the likes of the OK Corral.

Anyway, heads up, some of the classic characters from the first two books make some quick appearances in this, the third in the series, *Rio Grande Black Magic,* which covers the investigation into the assassination of Pancho Villa. Was Gunther there? If so, why would he help shoot Pancho Villa? General Blackjack Pershing is assigned by the US President to find out. Was the motive something that happened years back in the thwarted Villa raid of Tremboro, Texas on the Rio Grande? A time when Gunther, Jefe and others took a last stand? Or something way more? Like a lifelong vendetta?

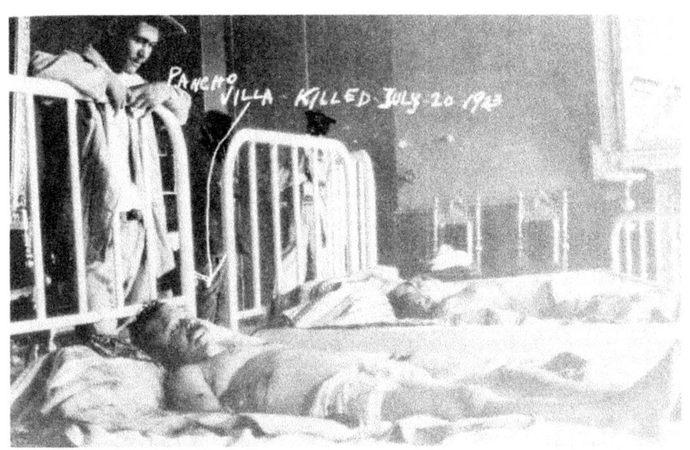

Chapter 1: The Expuesto of the Bone Breaker
August, 1924 Big Bend, Texas

"Villa?" the Mexican said solemnly. "That day he died?"

"That day," General Blackjack Pershing said.

"You cannot tell anyone about dis. What I tell you," the Mexican said, shifting in his seat. "If dey know I am alive? Dey will kill me!"

"We will report this to our government. The American government. The President of the United States only," General Pershing said.

The man shook his head and looked down on the tile floor of the Ft Bliss, Texas Provost Marshal's office. He was surrounded by seated Army officers, all taking notes but for the general, who sat before him, empty handed.

"No one in Mexico will know," General Pershing said.

"Mexico thinks I am dead. That I died that day. The day Villa died."

"And so shall that idea remain. This is a secret report."

"If dey know I am alive..."

"Who, sir?"

"The goberment. The Mexican goberment. Dey want to...to borrar..."

"Erase," a nearby seated Lt. Hawes translated.

"Si, *erase* me, anyone, anything with Villa. Gone. Olvi-dado."

"If you wish, we can find a way to move you. Way north."

"I don't know. I live now in Big Bend. I have a family. A shoe store dere, with my family."

"It is up to you," General Pershing said. "Tell us what happened."

"Villa. that day," the man said. "That day. De death in de streets. De shoosting, it did not happen like dey says in de newspapers. Dey only talk to Ramon. Dey think Ramon is the only survivor. Dey think I died."

General Pershing nodded. "Tell us why you were there that day."

"I was a bodyguard. My uncle was in Villa's army, and Villa kept him on after the war. My uncle knew I was a...you know...a tough hombre. I was once a wrestler in Mexico City. I was popular. My wrestling name was *Rompe Huesos*. 'Bone Breaker.' And, also...I had to do some tough jobs for de local mayors."

General Pershing nodded.

"So, too many of the Villa bodyguards were old like him?"

"My Uncle. Old, you know? And dey knew dey had to have younger, faster hombres. My uncle hired me to come to de Villa hacienda near Parral, Chihuahua. Villa turned the area into a military colony for many of his old soldiers. Then in 1923, as presidential elections approached. He...put him-self back into de Mexican politics." The man thrust a flat hand in the air like a knife.

He took a sip of the Army coffee. Pershing sipped his too.

"That time. Villa left all his bodyguards at home, except for seis...six...of us. Six men. Villa traveled to Parral, Mexico with just a few of us. He...he went to Parral very often. His young messtress was there. She was bery beautiful. Two days before, der was some baptism of a friend's baby he wanted to...to...see. But he stayed in Parral to be with the senorita."

He sat back in his chair. It was clear he regretted this recollection. He sighed, his eyes filled a bit, but he continued.

"Villa, he was driving de Dodge Roadster. With my uncle and Ramon and two other guards. I was in a second car, another Roadster behind him, with another hombre. His name was Savaco. He died that day too. As we drove, people in the streets saw Villa sometimes and yelled out his name. 'Viva Villa!' you know, they still say. 'Viva la Revolution!' They still say. Same with this day. His last day."

The man scratched his ear and shook his head side-to-side.

"Villa slowed down at de, de crossroads, de...you know...intersección of streets. At the road to Canutillo. Then! Then de men came out. De shoosters! The newspapers say seven shoosters. Who knows. Maybe seven? Lots of men came out from behind de corners of the buildings. Boaf leff and right side of us. Dey came shoosting the long guns. Rifle. Shotgun. One man had a machine gun. De Americano had this type of gun. De cars were almost stopped anyway and then de cars just...slowly rolled.

We tried to get out and get our guns up to shoost back."

"The American," Pershing said. "Tell me about him."

"He was...he was maybe 50? 55 years old? The baggy face of 55? Tall and tin. He had a flat brown hat, like your army, this kind of hat." He pointed to the general's hat on the side table.

"He had a brown leather jacket. He had ahhh, tan, you say...tan pants. Brown boots. He have the Americano machine gun. The Thompson machine gun that your army have, and he came walking sideways, shoosting into de car."

"Did he say anything?"

"He did not. He ...just keeps shoosting but at de first car. I am hoping he stops at de first car. The machine gun was...was...punching *big,* fast bullets into...de first car. I was asustado! And I am not a man of fear...easily...but I knew we were to be dead!"

"Yes."

"I...am shot. Here and here and here," the man pointed to his left arm, his right leg and chest.

"I fall from de car. The left side, back seat and I lost my pistola. I was...no hands - I mean no guns in my hands. I believe they did not shoost me no more because I had no guns, you know? Pancho Villa is shot too! He falls out of the car in front of me. Pancho is trying to sit up. He has no gun. The Americano walks up to him, de machine gun aimed at him. And Pancho says...like he is surprised to see him...he says, 'Johann! You too? You too, Johann?'"

"He said that? He said 'Johann?'" Pershing said.

"He say that. Yes."

"Johann. What did the American say?"

"He say nothing."

"He said nothing?"

"He say nothing. He just look. He look. Den he shoosts Villa in the chest. Villa falls over on de sidewalk. I think he is dead now for sure. The Americano waited for a segundo to look at him."

Pershing nodded.

"I crawl away. But de men, de shoosters' all ran away. Dey stop shoosting when Villa was shot again. There is a story that Villa said to Ramon, 'Don't let it end like this. Tell them, I did something.' Like Villa died a hero, you know? He wishes to die like de hero. But this is not true. Ramon is a liar. Ramon lived too, but today is already dead from something else. Maybe poison, people say. But, I think Villa was dead as I crawled away from de cars. My uncle was dead, though I did not think of him at the time. Some people on the street got me and carried me away. I...stayed with them. Hiding. I stayed a secreto because I believe that the Conspiración will kill me to end de story of Pancho Villa. They always end de problem with death in Mexico."

A lieutenant handed General Pershing an 8x10, black and white photograph. Pershing glanced at it. He rolled his chair closer to the man and handed him the photo.

"Is this the American?"

The man looked over the photo. It was of a hatless man, about 50, tall and somewhat thin.

"He could be. I do not know for sure."

"He could be? Take a real good look," Pershing said.

"I cannot say. Many Americans they, they look like this. They all look de same. Especially if they are old like this."

"His name is Johann. Johann Gunther," Pershing said.

"I...I don't know. I cannot tell. I cannot be sure."

"Are you afraid that you have to testify in court? Be..."

"Expuesto," the lieutenant beside Pershing said.

"No, I am not afraid," he lied.

"Why would an American help the Mexican government assassinate Pancho Villa?" Pershing said.

"I know not, Senior General."

The general took the photo back.

"Have you ever met, or do you know a Jesus Salas Barraza?" He handed the man another photograph.

He looked it over.

"I know of him. I have heard of him. I don't know him. He is de man that tells all de Mexico and Texas newspapers *he* killed Pancho Villa. Proud of it! But no one believes him. He goes to jail later for only 6 months and he is pardoned! Conspiración! Barraza becomes de..de.. how you say... responsible one. But what of de others? If he was de real asesino of someone like Villa...or de Presidente? Or de Governor? Dey would *torture* him." He clutched the fingers of his right hand with his left and twisted them, making an angry face. "Until he screams out de names of de odder shooters."

Pershing nodded.

"Big news it would be..ah, how you, say...trial! But with Villa? No torture for Barraza! Just 6 months! No one else is named. And dis phoney is set free." His hands went up and down in the air by his body. "Nothing broken on him. No torture. Conspiración!"

The man handed the photo of Barraza back.

"Am I...am I to remain a secreto?" the man asked.

"You are to remain a secret," the general lied.

Chapter 2: Dead End Tremboro
August 1924 Omaha, Nebraska

"We was at the end of the railroad line. As far as the old train could run. Tremboro, Texas. The Rio Grande fell next. A steep, steep, killing drop down to the river where we was. Then after that? It was, Mexico. Old Mexico. Mexico was in trouble again. Another revolution. Rio Grande or not. You know, a river ain't stopping no war. Just slowing it down till the bridges and the boats come. Huh, General? The killing. The propaganda. The pillaging. The destruction. The raids. River ain't stoppin' that," the fuzzy-headed, bug-eyed man said.

General Pershing nodded.

"My pappy saw the Red River once from the Oklahoma side. My pappy, he was from New Hampshire and he had no idea about size of things. The size of states. The size of Texas. You know, where Texas is on a map even. He didn't know. Exactly. Where Oklahoma is. He looked over the Red River in Oklahoma and asked me, 'That Mexico over there, Willin?'

'No Pappy. That's Texas, I said. You have to go a hunnert' days into Texas before you see the likes of Mexico.'

Granted it was a big view and we was high up. We could see afar. But, my pappy was, you might say, a geographic dumbass.”

“And so, you stopped at Tremboro,” Pershing said.

But when the train stopped at Tremboro Station, Texas, there was all kinds of trouble fer me, this strange gentleman Johann Gunther and his little Filipeenio islander, compadre named, or nicknamed ‘Jefe.’ Jefe means captain in Espanola so I don’t know if that was his real name or not? I don’t know about its meanings in Filipeenio, either. Nope. He looks Mexican, but he ain’t. He went to college in Madrid, Spain! Spain! Imagine that! And he’s a Mus-leum. He don’t believe in no Jesus Christ.”

Willin Calabash paused and looked around the room at the officers taking notes, waiting for their surprise. None came.

“He looks a little Chinese sometimes in the wrong light too. Gunther and Jefe were down there in Tremboro for guns. Various kinds of guns, mostly common pistols and some rifles they could carry back to Ft Worth and also for some bodyguard, protection job they got further east on the border out near the Gulf. They were hired to protect a family of whites, the Whittles, from the Mexes who wanted their land. You know that Plan de San Diego thing. They *never* quit, you know, General? Fightin’ amongst themselves. Fightin the border Texicans.

Gunther had these two Whittles teenagers with them from that family. Nice kids. Shiny-faced. Blondies. Their daddy wanted them to live a little. See the world. Have an adventure. Oh my God, what a mistake. What a mistake. He made Gunther take those two poor kids to Tremboro.” Calabash shook his head.

“But now, hear this, we had some very crispy hombres on that train’s dead end run. I counted 10. They be lookin’ like killers of an international sort. Sun drenched. Gruff. One was from Ireland. One from Canada. One from Portugal. All lookin to work. Lookin to kill. Lookin like I was, to jern’ up with the Mexican revolt. Even still, we had no idea we were all being transported into this dead end, a hell hole of mercenaries, revolutionaries, black marketeers and…witches. And that evil, crazy Pancho Villa, and his monster friend Fierro. And that other killer Venzula. White magic witches and black magic witches. Tremboro. Shit-fire. Hell fire. Dead end."

"Okay. Okay." Pershing put up a hand. "Let's start from the beginning, before that train ride. Now for the record, what is your full name?"

Lt Hawes turned a box machine on the office table, a box about the size and look of large wooden jewelry chest with a long tube. He turned it so that the black, metal tube with a flared ending faced Calabash. Hawes put a recording roll into the device.

"Like a player piano, I take it? You want me to...to talk into this end of the pipe here?"

"Yes, sir, if you will, not too close, but in the direction. It's an *Edison's Stenographer's Friend,*" Lt Hawes said.

"Edison's...Thomas...The light bulb, Edison...?"

"Yes, sir. The light bulb Edison."

"Edison's stenooo...you are catching my words in this pipe and you still need these people writin' my words too?" He pointed to two soldiers seated near him with pads of paper and pencils.

"Yes, sir. The men will write your words down too, in a shorthand."

"Short…hand…" He looked down at their hands.

"And this device is a cautionary…ah…device in case they make a mistake."

Pershing nodded at Calabash, for him to begin. Calabash nodded back.

"Okay, for the official record, my name is Calabash. Willin Calabash."

"William?" Lt Hawes asked.

"No, Willin. I was a twin. Two boys. My twin brother's name is Able. My Mom and Pap got the notion to call us Willin and Able."

"I see..."

Calabash smiled, "They was hopeful. It's true!"

"What were you doing in South Texas, at the Southern border, 14 years ago, back in 1910?" Lt Hawes asked.

"I's lookin fer work. There were handbills and advertisements in newspapers everywhere that the Mexican Revolution needed soldiers. They proclaimed they would pay extry' for experienced soldiers, and I was that. I was in the US Army! And I knew how to run a machine gun, which was advertised as a specialty they needed.

I had a small butcher shop in Nebraska, and when it ran broke...I was in the wrong neighborhood of poor folks to sell meat. More pitiful people always asking for scraps and free food and such than ever actually *bought* any meat. I got on the trains to get on down to the border. Left my wife and kids and that damn yoke of a butcher's store. I…I promised to send them money and all."

"When did you first meet Johann Gunther?"

"I met him and Jefe and these two Whittle boys in Ft Worth at the rail station."

"And how did you…did you suddenly just strike up a conversation?"

"Like a match. I axed them a question about the trains and Gunth said I was lucky. He said to just foller' them. They was going the same way. On down to San Antoine, right down to Tremboro. I axed him if he too was a going to join the REvolt. He said no. I axed him why you going? He said to a gun store. 'A gun store,' says I? I said 'theys' plenty of gun stores in Ft Worth.' He said yes there was, but he wanted Mexican guns. I said, 'oh.' Cus' I knew what they meant. I said, 'you must be a gun collector then.'

And he said, 'sorta.'

We stood on the platform waiting, but the train was running late and one of the workers shouted that we had a two full hours more to wait.

So, Gunther said, 'let's eat!' There was a French restaurant at the station. We all did. They were good company for a suppertime. He found out I was in the army in Oklahoma, and he was too. Way before me."

"Tell us about this Gunther," General Pershing said.

"Yes, sir. He's a pilgrim from Germany. He speaks German and very good American too. He spoke Germanian to some Germans at the rail station. He wears a German Luger pistol in a shoulder holster, and a big, knife and a squared-off, automatic pistol on his belt. Bullets come out a metal box you stick inside it like the rifle. He's a tall enough feller. Blondy hair. Looks like a guy smoking tobacco on a *Player's Navy Cut* cigarette poster. Cowboy clothes…but with a wiff of the big city style. I told you he hailed from Ft Worth at the time. He grins and laughs at things that are not jokes to me."

Pershing thought that was funny and smiled, further bewildering Calabash.

"He does things funny too. Like he dips his buttered bread into coffee, and he eats the bread...looking a damp dish rag. Little..."

"...idiosyncracies," the general added.

"Well, Gunther is no idiot. He may know some idiot's secrets, but he is no idiot with secrets."

"I mean, you mean, he has odd habits," the General said. Calabash nodded.

"Odd habits. He was also a lawsman in Paris," Calabash continued. "Not France, mind ya. Paris, Texas, a little berg way up yonder near Oklahoma and Arkansas. He was in the Army twice. In and out. And traveled the world doing Army stuff the second time, even when he wasn't in the Army. He told me flat out that he and Jefe solves people's problems, and sometimes I gather they need to poke a few guns around, crack open a few bullets and they need such things that cannot be tracked or traced. Like Mesican guns. They said there's new sciences to track and classify guns and
bullets. But, I am getting out of order…"

"He has a detective agency," Pershing said.

"Yes, sir. Called Remedies. Remedies Detective Agency."

"And you think he was a gunfighter? A killer?"

"Ahhh I don't know sir. He's a little bit of everything. Maybe? More than just a gunman?"

"He might be more?" Pershing asked, "As they say, a gun for hire? An...assassin?"

"Maybe? Maybe. But, he's more than that maybe. I think. He is too nice a feller to be a stone killer. I think if you asked him? He'd know how to fix up yer taxes too."

"Has he told you about...about assassinating anyone?"

"*No,* sir."

"But that is how you found Gunther…" Pershing said.

"Well, I found him on the platform of the railroad station."

"I mean this is how you *found* him…to...to be. To be like. Your description of him."

"Oh, yes, sir."

"Educated," Pershing said.

"Yes, sir. At your West Point."

"It's a fine description, Mr Calabash," Lt Hawes added.

"I thank you. Thank you."

"Who were these two boys again, for the record?" Lt Hawes asked.

"Gunther said they were hired to protect a family, like I said, the Whittles, out toward the Gulf, along the Tex-Mex border. He and Jefe were hiring a few men to do this, like a team, and they needed some extry guns for them. The dad wanted the boys to go with Gunther on a…on the gun-buying trip. An adventure, I guess. Huh? Learn em something new? Their two older brothers were in the Army. Gunther and Jefe were very much against the idea, Jefe told me later. But since the man was paying them a lot of money. Against Gunther's wishes, they took the young fellers for the adventure. Such was a terrible, terrible mistake."

"And who were the boys, for the record?"

"The Whittles. The older boy, 17, was Josh Whittle. The younger one, 15, was Whistler Whittle."

"Whistler?" Lt. Hawes asked.

"Yes, sir. Whistler. Like whistlin'," he whistled.

"Were they wearing guns?"

"They were both wearing guns. Revolvers and gun belts. Their daddy *ordered* them to. A real mistake, I think."

"Now, what happened when you first got to Tremboro?" Pershing asked.

"The train stopped...you know...and we all got out and like I said, the place looked fine from the station. It was all decorated for 'Día de los Muertos' time. You know 'Day of the Dead.' Mesican holiday. They call it a day but it's several days. People dressing up in skeleton costumes. Painted faces. Paper skeletons hanging everywhere. Dead Mesicans come back to visit on them days? I guess they visit America over the border if there are enough Mesicans living there. I guess ghosts will travel to see kin folk."

"So, the city was celebrating..." Lt. Hawes started to ask.

"Not yet. It was early. But it was decorated. We looked down the long main street. Nice in parts. Busted up in parts. Ya know it started out as a mining town. Quicksilver. Mercury. Which is like a damn poison. You don't want to get it on yer fingers, in yer eyes, ner' in yer gut. I know now.

There were side streets off the main avenue. But no Re-volt soldiers, coaches ner anyone at the station to help any of us to our hotels or nothing. Those other fellers, there to join up with the Re-volt, just walked on into town. They had suitcases and saddlebags. But Gunth and the boys had steamer chests. Three of um. Gunther grabbed one end of one. Jefe grabbed the other end and with his other hand, he grabbed the handle of the second. I got the other end of that one. It was light! Empty. The two boys got the ends of the last one. We damn near stretched across the street in a line. We marched downtown. I don't know where the hotels were, but Gunther and Jefe knew. They were there before. That's when…that's when...we met the first witch…"

****

October 1915 Tremboro, Texas

"STOP!" An Hispanic woman shouted and stepped right in front of them, mid-street, one dirty hand held high, palm toward their advance. Bald. Middle-aged. Dirty long dress. Shoeless. Several rings ladened every finger. Her palm had a large tattoo on it, a design of circles and triangles. Her face was partially painted in a half-skeleton, in the Day of the Dead tradition.

"Stop! Go no further. This is a village of doom for you. Go back to your cities. Back to your homes. Back to your churches. Back to America!"

"Lady, I don't know where you think you are? But this here's America, right here," Calabash said.

Three other women stood nearby with serious expressions and painted faces, wearing long dresses and jackets with hoods. The men could still see parts of their bald heads underneath their hoods.

Gunther, Jefe, Calabash and the Whittle teens remained in their long line of luggage, but they did stop because she stood in front of them. The other men from the train split up and walked around them and the woman. The women backed up trying to garner their attention too.

"Hello, Celesta," Gunther said.

One man spit in her direction.

"Melt off, witch!" another man yelled.

"Ha, yeah," said another.

"Lady come on, you are telling us what?" Calabash asked

"Your future here, when you come here, you mix your futures into the futures that are here." Both her hands started swirling in circles.

"Like a…like a roulette wheel?" Calabash asked, his eyes circling to follow her hands.

"The futures must not mix. Like a tornado, it will tear you apart and send you into pieces, into the seven winds."

Page 22

She looked at the two teenagers.

"Especially you two bebes'! Stop. Go back," she said.

"Do not listen to her!" another woman's voice came from the distant right, "She is a witch."

"YOU are the witch!" Celesta, the bald woman yelled back.

"She is a witch of fear." This other woman approached them. Long black hair. Spanish. Beautiful. In a dress, also, but clean. Boots. Thick necklaces. "She runs out like this to everyone that gets off the train. She is loco in la cabesa."

Then, the four more attractive women with her stepped into the street. They were also dressed in newer, cleaner black dresses, black gloves, and wore thick makeup, unlike Celesta's band.

"This is not true," the bald woman said. She turned to the men, and stared at Calabash and the boys. "I do not run off anyone who comes. Only you. Only this day?" She pointed to the boys and Calabash.

"Only...?" Calabash said. "Ya mean like me? Are you talking to me? What about them?" He pointed to Gunther and Jefe.

"Not to them. I know them. To you, and you, and you. Bebes," she said, then she stared at the teens.

"Who are these women?" Calabash asked out loud in exasperation.

"Witches," Gunther said, as he started the luggage line moving forward again.

"WITCHES!" Calabash repeated.

"Mangkukulam," Jefe whispered, which is Filipino for witch.

The bald woman stood fast. As the luggage line approached her though, she leapt into the air like an acrobat, with a yelp, over the trunk between Gunther and Jefe. She cleared the luggage and landed behind all of them.

"I cannot protect you!" Celesta screamed.

"This is finally some truth from her. She cannot do anything," the other witch said.

"Witches," Gunther said to Jefe. "And they have never stopped us like this before. This is peculiar."

Jefe nodded.

They walked on, leaving the two witches to argue, and their two teams glaring at each other.

"We have been here four times buying guns," Gunther said to Calabash. "There are two churches of witches here. Good witches. Bad witches."

"Churches of witches?" Calabash said. "Whew! Which one is the good witch?"

"The bald one," Jefe said. "Her name is Celesta."

"Celesta the bald witch. And the delicious looking one is a bad witch, then? Ain't that the way."

"That's Zamora," Jefe said, "and they do Black Santa Muerta."

"Black Santa Muerta," Calabash repeated. "Ain't never heard of that."

"Spanish for *Our Lady of Holy Death*. To kill a man," Gunther said, "all you need is a black cloth doll, some thread, a human bone of some kind. Maybe even a toad. You may need a piece of metal the man held for a while. You must ask the Devil for permission, in person, at a cave in the hills where Satan lives."

"Reckon they must know where Satan lives. Caves," Calabash mumbled, looking back at the bald woman. "But she won't kill us right? What about the deee-licious one?"

"That delicious one you speak of? Zamora?" Jefe said. "That is not a woman. That is a man dressed as one. He is a warlock."

"No. NO! Thank you fer telling me. Oh my God. It's a man! Five minutes in this place and men are women and my soul is gonna' mix with a tornada'."

Gunther chuckled.

Calabash looked behind him and saw the two women, well the man and woman arguing, their faces inches apart.

"Blackened Santa Mutta," Calabash said.

"Muerta," Jefe corrected.

"Sounds like a drink. They got this Muerta back where you are from in Chinese Mexico?"

"The Philippines," Jefe said. "No, they have Allah and Jesus."

"Well, I know Jesus at least. Whew. But I guess everybody knows the Devil. He's everywhere, not just in a cave."

They marched down the dirt street in their long line of men, teens and steamers until they arrived in the town center with black paved streets. Most of the other men had filtered off into various hotels and eateries.

"We'll go down to that last one. The La Contessa," Gunther said.

"This here steamer is awful light," Calabash said.

"It is empty. We will fill it with Mexican guns," Jefe said.

"Well, hell, si Senor," Calabash said.

"I've never been called a 'bebe' before," Whistler said.

"It means, baby," Jefe said.

"I'm no baby," Whistler said, as he noted that the dirt road ended just ahead and the paved roadway began. He smiled big, stopped for a second, put his feet together and jumped onto the paved part, like a kid jumping into a lake. Jefe enjoyed that.

"Suppose we'll see those witches again?" Calabash asked.

"Probably will," Gunther said.

"Were all those witches in the nice black dresses, all...men too?" Calabash asked, looking over his shoulder at the squabbling group.

"Don't know," Gunther said.

"Why do men wanna' dress up like women?" Calabash asked.

"Don't know," Gunther said.

Jefe had a much longer answer, opened his mouth, but decided to take a pass on it, especially with the boys present.

The men and boys entered the La Contessa Hotel, released their steamers onto the carpeted floor. A middle-aged man sat in a chair at the end of the counter, legs spread wide apart. Atop a white apron was a giant bowl. The bowl was full of skinned peaches and getting higher by the hand maneuver. The man grinned as he carved the skin off a peach. He threw the skin into a bucket beside him. He looked up with that same smile.

"Looky here," the man said.

"Four, Mr Renkowitz," Gunther said.

"Yes, Mr Gunther. We've received your telegram."

"And I, your confirmation."

Renkowitz set the bowl on the counter, wiped his hands on his apron and stood. The Whittle boys wandered over to the peaches and the skins.

"You boys hungry?" he asked. "The peaches are for pies tonight but the skins ain't a going nowhere. And they can be scrumptious if I cut a bit too deep. Don't mind the bucket. It's clean. Dig in."

The boys did. Even Jefe grabbed a slice up, inspected it, then ate it.

"Hey Renk, do you have a room for another friend?"

"No, fraid not. Maybe you have heard? The got-dang Mexican Revolution people are here. They are recruiting for the Revolt. Most rooms are taken in town."

"Josh and I can bunk up in one room," Whistler said between bites. "Let Mr Calabash have a room."

"Thanks, boys, that's mighty swell of ya," Calabash said.

"Okay then," Renkowitz said.

"Does Rock Candy Randy still work here?" Gunther asked, shoving some Day of the Dead skull decorations aside to spin the log book around. One head was a small ashtray.

"Yes. Yes, he does. Helps out. His momma just died though."

"Oh no," Gunther said. "What's he...where is he living then?"

"He's got a back room, a shed really, at a woman's house. She knew his mother. About three blocks from here."

At that moment, a tall, skinny teenager walked into the lobby. He had red hair and an odd face, worn blue jeans, bad old boots and red plaid shirt.

"Nello, Nister Nunther," the boy said, seeing Gunther but not looking him in the eyes.

"Hello Randy," Gunther said.

"Nello, Nister Nefe."

"Buenas dias, Randy," Jefe said.

Jefe walked to him and shook his hand, and the boy grinned at that, which was hard as his face was contorted.

"We are sorry to hear about your madre."

The hard attempt at a smile disappeared.

"I don't nunderstand why," he said.

"No one does understand these things, Randy. How's school?" Gunther asked.

"Oh, I non't go to school no more. It's a bag of holes and troubles."

"How come?"

"They non't know where to put me. What grade. I non't know."

Gunther frowned. "The kids give you trouble?"

Randy stared at the floor and shrugged his shoulders.

"I can't keep him in the school house," Renkowitz said.

"He needs a special teacher and...and they don't have one. Nor a room for special kids. Nor the right books."

Gunther nodded.

"Nile help you with these newtcases," Randy said.

"Rooms 10, 11, 12, 13," the manager said, and Randy began towing the steamers up the stairs.

Josh and Whistler Whittle stared hard and quizzical at Randy, eyeing him up and down, not unnoticed by Jefe.

Jefe explained, "Randy's family was poor and since he was 7 years old, he's worked in the mercury mines out here. A lot of the children work in the mines here, you know. Money. It's a terrible place and many of them die or get sick."

"Quicksilver," Josh said.

"Yes. Mercury. Quicksilver. Cinnabar. The doctors say, it's very dangerous. You cannot really touch it!" Jefe said. "You cannot touch it without the danger of the poison. It is a special poison that glows in the air, but you cannot really, easily see any glow. You cannot smell it. It is inside things like thermometers."

"That sounds like magic," Whistler said.

"It is. If it is magic? It's in the air like electricity or the mystery of the radio. The mystery of electricity. It does not bother all the people, but it hurts many. They say, Randy was always touching and playing with the mercury down in the mines. Without gloves. This is how he got the nickname Rock Candy Randy. Some say he even put it in his mouth sometimes."

"Crazy, huh, Jefe?" Josh said. "It must taste horrible."

"He was only seven. By the time Randy was 11," Jefe continued, "his...his brain...was not...working right. His body too. You...you saw him."

The boys listened intently. Their ranch lives, their ranch friends and ranch families knew nothing of such mines and what they might do to people.

Rock Candy Randy returned to the lobby for more steamers, and Gunther changed the subject.

"Where's the Revolution recruiting set up?" he asked.

"In the Rotunda Restaurant."

"Right across the street! Remind me not to go here," He spun the registration book back to face Renkowitz.

Also on the counter was a bowl of nuts and a glass jug of water. Lemons floated with the ice cubes. Gunther grabbed a glass and opened the spicket.

"Boys, getcha' some lemon water too. It's been a dusty trail."

The two teens stepped over and grabbed glasses.

"Can you fly a plane?" Renkowitz asked. "Because you know the revolutionaries will pay a ton of money to pilots," the clerk said.

"None of us can fly a plane," Gunther said.

"Perhaps you have heard of Pancho? Pancho Villa?" Renkowitz asked the boys..

The boys snapped wide eyed toward the clerk while drinking.

"Oh yes," Gunther said. "They have."

"The Generalissimo himself is here! And some of his men. Collecting mercenaries and guns," Renkowitz said as he handed Gunther all the room keys. "News is they are on the run again from the Federales.

"That must be the tornada we heard about," Calabash said. "I did not expect Pancho Villa himself to be here doing the recruiting."

"Tornado?" Renkowitz asked.

"Yeah, the witchy-woman with the bald head told us about a tornado."

"Celesta? Already?"

"Yeah," Gunther said, "she was the welcoming party at the train station. Zamora showed up too. I reckon they're busy, Day of the Dead and all."

"It's always days and days of the dead for them," Renkowitz said, shaking his head.

Jefe shook his head too. "Maybe we should come back next week?"

"I am seriously thinking about it," Gunther said, as he handed out the room keys.

"How are their churches?" Gunther asked.

"Busy," Renkowitz said. "They pull those poor Mexicans in. And we know some of the white women even go on Sundays. They're all praying and singing and casting their spells. And, needless to say, donating. It's always a competition with which one is the bigger church."

Gunther nodded.

"I should caution you," Renkowitz said. "El Carnicero is here with Villa. The Butcher. Rudolfo Fierro. Stay out of his sight. Do not even cast eye balls upon him. He is a crazed dog who will kill anyone. Over any thing. Just to test out his bullets. You know he will put people in a line to see how many people his bullets will shoot through. And…and…Emile Venzula. He's here too. Emile wants to be Pancho's new Butcher man. If Fierro doesn't kill him first. There is already trouble between them."

"El Carnicero," Josh said, "what's that mean?"

"Butcher," Jefe answered.

"Muchas gracias Senior," Gunther said to Renkowitz. "We will certainly worry over these men and names."

Renkowitz rapped his knuckles on the counter.

They left the counter area, bound for the stairs.

"Thank you, Randy," Gunther said.

"Yes, thanks," the boys both said, still confused about Rock Candy Randy's condition and watched him closely, maybe to catch a quicksilver glow spot on him somewhere?

"You are welcome," Randy said, looking at them for just a second, then bowing his head.

Gunther stopped suddenly at the stairs, turned and said, "Hey, Renk, the witches. Why did one stop us on the street? That's never happened before. What do you think?"

"The witches? They are fighting like cats and dogs. It's because of these new men here and Pancho Villa. The black magic warlock Zamora, the *Black* Santa Muerta wants to work for Pancho. Advise him in the battles. Villa can be very superstitious."

"He has a history," Gunther said.

"Is he listening to them?" Jefe asked.

"I don't know. I am just keeping to myself about it all."

As they got to the rooms, they saw their luggage stacked by the doors. Jefe advised the boys, "I would keep the door locked. I would not go outside alone. In about an hour we'll visit the gun store."

"Yes sir," Whistler said. Excited, they got their steamer and hustled in to see their room.

"They have never been in a hotel before," Jefe said.

Gunther, Jefe and Calabash stood in the hall.

"It truly stinks of trouble here, Gunth," Jefe said. "You have once again, like with all your women, terrible timing."

"I sure do. We need outta' here as soon as we can."

"Well, I'm here for a piece of that RE-volt action," Calabash said. "And I'll meet the one and only Pancho Villa to boot! Whhooooo doggies!"

With that resounding wail, Gunther and Jefe remained expressionless and silent. They turned, grabbed the handles of
their steamers and entered their rooms.

Chapter 3: Ten Candles and a Stick a Dynamite
August 1924, Omaha, Nebraska

"We settled ourselves in the hotel with the idea of going to the gun store in an hour. When we did, what a place! And they sold musical instruments right there too. A Chinaman owned the shop. I tell ya, General, within a few hours we saw everyone. Like a opera house grand troupe. We saw Pancho Villa. We saw Fierro the Butcher. We saw Emilio Venzula, who I think was crazier than hell, and a damn sight worse than Fierro. I mean we saw everyone you ever wanted to hate within a few hours," Calabash said.

"Did you get the idea this was the first time Pancho Villa and Gunther met?" Blackjack Pershing asked.

"Oh I think it's the first time. Monumental, huh? I mean those two are what we are here for, huh?"

"I am not sure…monumental is the right word, Willin," the general said.

"Well, I think it is. Don't you fellers?" he looked around the room. "History in the making. Wait till you hear what happened next!" Calabash said.

****

October 1915, Tremboro, Texas

Gunther, Jefe and Calabash stood outside the Whittle boys' hotel door. Jefe knocked. Whistler opened the door and the three men walked in.

"Bout' ready?" Gunther said.

Jefe stared at the cowboy hat on one of the beds.

"Whose hat is this?" Jefe asked.

"Mine," Whistler said, pulling on his jacket.

"You know, it is bad luck to put your hat on a bed?" Jefe said.

"Huh?" Whistler said.

"And it is not upside down." Jefe picked up the hat. "The hat must rest upside down with the crown on the bottom. If you lay your hat down on the brim, the flatness will reshape your brim and make it flat. You will become ugly to the ladies."

Both teens stared at Jefe.

Calabash also stood with his jaw down listening.

"It is bad luck for the cowboy to have a hat on a bed, especially a rodeo cowboy and usually when someone else puts it there," Jefe said. "To lose this case of bad luck, you have to spit in the hat, throw the hat on the ground and stomp on the hat. If you wish to win the rodeo."

"I ain't gonna do all that," Whistler said. "That sounds like a big ol' superstition. And I like that hat! And I don't aim to be in a rodeo, Jefe."

Jefe smiled, "I know Whistler, I am just telling you the ways of the American cowboy."

"Jefe had to go all the way to college in Madrid, Spain, to learn the ways of the American cowboy," Gunther said.

The boys looked back at Jefe.

"Jefe belonged to a college group that studied the American West and the American cowboy," Gunther said. "When he was in college in Madrid, Spain. As a hobby. Then he met me and learned the truth about what a mess we are."

Jefe grimaced. "This is true," he said.

The boys laughed, They all left the room.

"You ever put your hat on the bed, Mr Gunther?" Whistler whispered as they left.

"Never," Gunther whispered back.

Chueng's Guitar and Gun Store was a brick, metal and wood, two-story building, mid-street with empty lots on either side for horses, and cars to park. Hi "High" Chueng immigrated from Hong Kong to San Francisco in 1898. While working odd jobs in Chinatown, he ran afoul with various Chinese gangs. He didn't want to pay them a percentage of his pay checks. But Chueng observed that the gangs always needed a steady flow of ammo, guns and explosives. "High" Chueng had Oriental friends at the docks, and he began a small network of importing caches of knives, guns and bomb parts from South America for the gangs. Other customers soon followed (even some local police departments needed the very same supplies at cut rates).

Then, Chueng caught wind of the Mexican Revolution and decided to escape the growing politics and pressures (and gang shootings) of the Bay Area and move way southeast. First to Laredo, but he wound up on his own developed "Silk Road" of Tremboro, Texas, establishing his own trail of Central, South and North America, gun running for various people and groups, thanks to the railroad.

But Hi "High" Chueng's first love, was always music, and he was a real master of the guitar. He loved it, and all stringed instruments. Since he constructed and owned his own store, he turned the place into both a music shop *and* a gun store. Americans and Mexicans for miles around visited this establishment to purchase the finest guitars and any and all quantities of pistols and rifles. In 1904, Gunther and Jefe delivered an order of expensive, sought-after, European, Brilldon Guitars to this outpost from the Galveston docks. These were handmade instruments that many Houston businessmen and collectors were after too. During this delivery, a raider had to be shot and killed. This delivery by Gunther and Jefe put Tremboro on the map for musician business, and made Remedies trusted friends of the shop.

Gunther's little posse of men and boys crossed some Tremboro avenues and side streets to get to Chueng's. On this fall day, the two vacant lots beside the store were almost full with waiting horses, carriages and cars. There was a large open bus, its driver bored and smoking a pipe sitting on its doorstep. A doorman in clean, pressed pants and shirt, and a short brim, straw hat stood at the front door, looking around. A gun store in these parts needed an armed doorman, though as in most places such as this one, they were opening fire, cannon fodder for sneaky armed robbers. The doorman smiled brandishing some good teeth, and wearing a pistola on his hip as he opened one of the two front doors.

"Thank you, sir," Gunther said.

They filed inside the place. Bright electric lights. Wooden walls, peppered with furs and paper posters of guns, men huntin,' men with knives wrastlin' with bears, snakes and crocs, ladies with a lot of shoulder and kneecap showing, holding up rifles. Posters of guitars too. Full of folks looking at the musical instruments on one side and guns on the other. Gunther, Jefe and Calabash recognized some of the customers were the Villa recruits they rode in with hours earlier. Some were Mexican soldados with Villa's group. Some were Texas music lovers. Others, area hunters and shooters.

The boys immediately spotted the color posters of short-skirted, women holding guns. The ladies' hair flowed loose and windswept wild. The boys' jaws actually dropped. Gunther smiled, but Jefe, ever the prude, was concerned.

"Now boys, BOYS!" Jefe said.

"Sir?" Josh said.

"You will disturb yourself by looking at such pictures. Eyes away!" Jefe barked. "Eyes away."

"This one," Gunther said with a wry smile, "looks like a girl I knew from..."

"Oh, I am sure you did know her. One of thoughtless and meaningless sex," Jefe complained.

An old man with a beard sat on a stool in a far corner and played a guitar and sang. Many of the stern men on the train were there wandering around. The tough demeanor of some gone, now with softer eyes and smiles as they heard the light music and caressed the guitars, ukuleles and violins.

> *"Be my little baby bumble bee,*
> *Buzz around, buzz around, keep a-buzzin' 'round.*
> *Bring home all the honey, love, to me,*
> *Little bee, little bee, little bee."*

A scruffy giant of a man in a duster and two-gun belt picked up a guitar and strummed several cords, than quickly turned to the singer and said gingerly, "Oh, I am sorry, sir."

The singer stopped, "On, no problem, sir," and he waited for the big man to fully test the strings. "This is a guitar store, sir, and you are king."

High Chueng spotted Gunther and Jefe, and approached them from around the counter.

"Weeelll, look at what the bobcat brought in!" He shook Jefe's hand first then Gunther's.

"Who you running with here?" High Chueng asked, and Gunther introduced Calabash and the Whittle boys.

"High, You are a bit busy today," Gunther said.

"Yes, yes, we are. The Revolution recruiters are all here," Chueng said. "New recruits. And the recruiters like guns and music."

"All ya need is the whiskey and beer," Gunther said.

"I thought about it. I thought about it, but it can get crazy enough in here sometimes. We had a gunfight right in that corner over there. Two Laowais…"

Calabash looked dumfounded at the foreign word, his bushy eyebrows about collapsed down on his face.

"Ah, Laowais," Chueng shook his head, "Chinese word for you...you white, pale people. A guy from Kansas. Guy from Alabama. What started the spat? Your Civil War? Better gun? Best bullet? Got to be who shoulda' won the War. I don't know. They shot each other in the arm. Ba-aaa-m. If I start to sell whiskey in here? We'd all be dead in a month. Marshal Heston would put *me* in jail."

Chueng pointed at the front corner opposite the singer. There on an elevated wooden platform some 5 feet up sat a giant man with long black hair and beard with a double bar-reled shotgun across his lap. He had a big table there too.

"That's my man, Hercules."

"Hercules," Gunther repeated. "He looks like a Hercules."

"That is his Christian name, though it might sound like it comes from Greek mythology. Hercules. How his mamma knew he would grow that damn big some day, is some kind of magic."

Chueng rolled a thumb over, pointing to the far counters, nodding his head to the right side. Gunther and his group turned. Right there, stood the one and only General Pancho Villa at one end of a long gun case, sans his big hat, which laid atop the glass. Brow side down, a violation of the cow-boy code.

"He's gonna have him a bad hat look," Whistler said to Jefe.

Jefe grinned back at him.

"He told me that he is going to buy a lot of guns, but not all the guns. We will have guns for you," Chueng said.

Villa was in conversation with the warlock Zamora. Zamora was dressed to the nines like a beautiful woman in a sweeping, long dress. Villa touched his/her shoulder with a giant smile at one point, and he rested a hand on that shoul-der. He/she giggled. Gunther smirked at this as he strolled the displays of pistols.

Zamora left the store with some coy over-the-shoulder looks back at Villa, as if on a sudden mission for him. With idle shopping, Gunther suddenly found himself beside the General when Villa wandered his way around also looking at the firearms.

The singer kept singing -

> *"Let me spend the happy hours,*
> *Roving with you amongst the flowers,*
> *And when we get where no one else can see,*
> *Cuddle up, cuddle up, cuddle up,*
> *Be my little baby bumble bee,*
> *Buzz around, buzz around, keep a-buzzin round,*
> *We'll be just as happy as can be,*
> *You and me, you and me, you and me."*

Without looking up at Villa, Gunther said, "You know that woman is a man?"

"De woman…" Villa repeated.

"…is really a man. That is a man dressed as a woman."

Villa smiled broadly, turned to Gunther and his head leaned back for a better look at Zamora.

"I would not get too close with her. Him," Gunther said.

"My English is not perfecto, Senior. You are saying that Zamora, under the vestir, is not a senorita?"

"Si, Generalissimo. She...he is a Senior."

Villa called two of his men over and they spoke. They laughed.

"Hohahahahh," Villa laughed again. He looked down again at the guns. "I can see Senior, what you are talking about now. Yes, yeees. I can see. De face, under de...you know...de... face paint, it looks like a skinny hombre!"

"A man such as yourself, known to…to love a woman… should continue to love only women."

"Haaahahaha," Villa laughed this time quietly.

They looked at the guns.

"So Senior…?"

"Gunther. Johann Gunther."

"From…Germany? I can tell by de name."

"Once, but now from Ft Worth, Texas. But yes, 25 some odd years ago or so. From Germany."

"Ahhh. And you…you…you…you…you are here in Tremboro, to enlist in the Revolution?"

"Ah, no Generalissimo. I am only here to buy some guns."

"You look like a soldier," Villa looked Gunther over. He made two fists and shook them a little in the air to suggest a certain virility. "Where you once a soldado?"

"Once. But when I was a soldier, I did not look like one. Now that I am not one anymore, I look like one."

Villa pondered that. The language."Yeees, I see what you say. Ha!"

"It is a curse, of a kind," Gunther said. "To look like something you are not."

"And to act as such, Yes?" Villa said. He put on his hat.

"Certainly so. Yes."

"Like dis man who looks like a woman," Villa declared.

"Exactamente," Gunther said with a chuckle.

"Ohhh, but dis is a bad time for you to buy guns, Senior Gunther. I possess many pesos to buy all the guns in Chueng's store."

Gunther just let that remark go by.

Chueng stepped up, nervous by expression and tone, "Yes, Johann, The General has plans to buy most of the… guns."

"And the guitars, too?" Gunther said.

"Haaah!" Villa laughed. "We only have a small use for the guitars…but the guuunns. The guns. Or maybe…maybe the guitar cases because we can hide the big guns in them and get close to de Patrones we must shoot."

A well-dressed, Mexican walked up to them and asked Gunther, "Do you fly planes?"

"You are the second man today to ask me that question," Gunther said.

"This is my amigo and my Major, Emilio Venzula," Villa said.

"Major," Gunther said with a nod, "But, no sir, I cannot fly a plane."

"Do you know of any Americanos that can fly planes?"

Gunther faked a serious few seconds of serious thought.

"No, I can't say that I do."

"Una pena," Venzula said.

"It is a pity," Gunther confirmed.

Venzula was as tall as Gunther, thinner, too handsome, and with a charm Gunther immediately distrusted. There was a layer of cruelty he could sense. He did not dress like a soldier.

"Who else has asked?" Venzula said.

"The clerk at my posada," Gunther said, "telling me that if I flew a plane, you would pay me a lot of money."

"Haaa! Oh, dat' we could. We would," Villa said.

"There are two boys with you. The two Blondies. They are…your sons?" Villa asked.

"No, they are the sons of a friend."

"Ahh, I ask because of the rubia hair. Are they buying guns?"

"They are here only to travel. To see the world."

"The world of Texas," Villa said. "I see that they are wearing guns."

"Yes," Gunther said showing his reluctance. "They are young. They wanted too. Their father made me let them. I hope I can keep them alive, minute to minute."

Villa leaned in to whisper, "some of my men, not the Americans coming to see me, but some of my men would like those nice guns and their nice holsters. You take care of them, hey?"

"I wish they were fake guns," Gunther said. He knew to make a joke after the veiled threat. It was a threat, not a helpful warning.

"Yes! Fakes! What a surprise it would be huh? If something were to happen to them, and my men tried to shoot dose guns…and SORPRISA! They are toys huh?"

"What a surprise," Gunther repeated with a smile.

"Like reaching…reaching down into the pants of Zamora and finding a pecker there, huh?" Villa said, and laughed again.

"Tonight. Come to eat with us tonight. At the Rotunda.

Seven o'clock? Si? I need some smart people to talk to. Where are you staying?"

"The Contessa," Gunther said, and quickly regretted it.

"You are at the Contessa? I will have Emilio escort you safely through these streets, because there are many crazy people here, no?"

Emilio Venzula nodded. "Many…crazy…people," Venzula repeated.

"The Contessa is right across the street from the Rotunda," Gunther said.

"Chueng will be there, and he will play for us. Chinese music. Mexican music and Americano music. Heeeey?"

"Si, Generalissimo," Chueng shouted back.

"See you later, Senor Johann Gunther," Villa said.

Gunther looked over more of the guns as Jefe and Calabash approached him.

"Dinner at seven," Gunther said.

"No!" Jefe said, still in a whisper.

"I think I have to go. Venzula will escort me."

"I will go too."

"No, you won't."

"Well, I will be there. You are not going alone. I will go ahead."

"I know I can't stop you," Gunther said while looking over the guns.

"Be like sitting at a rickety table with 10 candles and a stick a dynamite," Calabash said. "That dude is a little creepy to me. Just lookin at em."

"That's your new boss," Gunther said.

"Should we buy the guns now? The train does not leave until tomorrow," Jefe said.

"I hate to have 40 guns in our hotel rooms with these bands of out-runners all about," Gunther said. "They may hunt us down. Maybe we'll buy them first thing in the morning and get out of here?"

"This place is trouble," Jefe said.

"Tornado of souls," Gunther muttered.

Calabash's eyes widened at the prophesied word, "tornado." The singer sang on -

> *"We'll be just as happy as can be*
> *You and me, you and me, you and me.*
> *Honey, keep a-buzzin, please,*
> *I've got a dozen cousin bees,*
> *But I want you to be my baby bumble bee*
> *Buzz-buzz."*

Chapter 4: Fine Dining and Death with Pancho Villa
August 1924 Omaha, Nebraska

"Jefe and I went to the bar to eat but we did not sit close to Gunther and Villa. What they said exactly, I don't know, but Gunther told me later, and then even more later again," Calabash told the officers.

"They appeared to be...friendly?" Pershing asked.

"So far. A whole lot happened that we all could see and hear though. Whew. Arguments. Threats. Almost a castration right there at the big dinner table."

"A...castration?" Pershing said. "A...bulls?"

Calabash chopped his hand in the air. "A woman! I mean a man. Balls off!"

All the steno officers looked up with raised eyebrows.

****

October 1915 Tremboro, Texas

At 6:45 p.m., Gunther left his room for the restaurant. Jefe and Calabash left for the restaurant at 7 p.m. The two stopped at the hotel counter.

"We have those two boys in 11," Jefe said. "They'll need something to eat soon."

"The wife is making a potato casserole tonight," Renkowitz said. "We can get them fed."

"Muchas gracias," Jefe said.

Gunther made it a point to be there early, to be there *before* Venzula was supposed to "escort" him over to the restaurant. He walked in to quite a crowded community affair - about 30, well-groomed men and women. Four long dinning tables in the center of the room. And the guest of honor was Pancho Villa. On Gunther's closer inspection, the guests appeared to be either citizens of Tremboro or new recruits for the revolution.

"Here, here, Senor Gunther, sit next to me! Por favor," Villa said, waving his hand.

Not his first choice, wishing to sit quietly anywhere else and observe, he approached the appointed chair slowly. There were about 10 people seated at this one long table. Two men, obvious bodyguards, stood sternly about 15 feet back from the Generalissimo. A man sat in a chair just behind Villa and to his right.

"Yes, please. Dis is me amigo, Rudy. He helps me to translate." He pointed to the man to his left, who nodded at Gunther.

"Yes. Yes. Senor Chueng tells me, that you are a graduate of de West Point," Villa said.

"I am."

"How you do dat? A poor German boy goes to West Point?"

"Well, General, I was in the army, cavalry at first, as many poor people must do."

"Oh? Yes, I know."

"Got out...of the Army, and became a deputy in north Texas...in Paris, Texas."

Rudy translated.

"Yes...yes, a lawman. But Texas has such a city named like in France?" Villa asked.

"Yes. And there was a group there...the Klu Klux Klan...killing people..."

"Yes. I know of these people. Oh my. Terrible people."

"It's a long story, but I solved the murders. Some of the murders happened in Oklahoma too, and the Governor of Oklahoma knew my life was in danger from the KKK in Texas..."

Rudy helped translate.

"Yes, from the Klu Klux Klan!"

"And he arranged for me to attend West Point. Up, way up in New York State. For almost 4 years."

"Dis is an amazing story. The Klu Klux Klan. Dis is a bery bad group because they hate all Mexicans and all de negros."

Rudy helped translate.

Villa sipped his lemonade, the contents of the glass caught Gunther's eye.

"I do not drink de alcohol," Villa added, "So, a Major...? Lieutenant? Colonel? What was your rank in the Army?"

"A mere Major," Gunther said.

"A mere Major. Not so mere. And you left the army again..."

"For money. To do other work that paid me better," Gunther said. "Sometimes...sometimes the same work, for much better money."

"Ahhhh HAAA. De soldier for hire. This is good news to me, 'Mayor Militar' Gunther. What kind of work?"

"Oh, problem solving. Solving people's problems."

"You know, Major, de Revolution is a big problem for people. Guillermo, some wine for Major Gunther," Villa ordered a man dressed in a white suit like a cook, or a chef that was standing nearby.

"Red," Gunther told Guillermo.

"Ladies and Gentlemen!" a corpulent man in a black suit stood and shouted. Everyone stopped talking. "We are honored here tonight to have as our Guest of Honor, Generalissimo Pancho Villa, hero of the Mexican Revolution."

Everyone clapped. There was even a whistle or two. Villa raised his lemonade and smiled that face-splitting grin of his.

"We all support the Revolution in Mexico. Tonight, we invite him to see our Day of the Dead Parade, which will pass right by this restaurant in a few hours."

More clapping. The speaker sat and the conversation returned to normal.

"Your friend," Villa pointed to Jefe as he and Calabash walked into the bar. "Your friend is Mexican?"

"Filipino. From the Philippines. We met and became friends in the war there."

"And you remain compadres?"

"Hermanos."

"Ahhh, hermanos." Villa stared at Gunther's face, liking that answer. That a white man would become brothers with a Hispanic man. "I do not know the details of this war, but I hope it was for a good cause?"

Gunther did not know how to answer that one. He looked down at his newly arrived red wine.

Zamora, the warlock/witch, woman/man walked into the restaurant, resplendent in a black dress, causing whispers and serious faces. Villa stood up.

"Ohhhhh, PLEEZ, pleez you have a seat here, here," Villa said with that big smile. Zamora did.

"Senors and senoritas, I have an announcement!" Pancho said loudly with a big grin. Now he stood. He took his fork and dinged it on the side of his glass. "PLEEZ!"

Everyone quieted almost immediately.

"It seems we have a surprise guest, tonight. Or should a say a guest…with a surprise! It seems, I am told by my good amigo, Major Johann Gunther, that…that a guest here is not as she seems," Villa said.

Gunther squirmed in his seat just a bit.

"It seems dat the senorita Zamora, dis…dis beautiful creature beside me here…is really…a MAN!"

Everyone from Tremboro already knew this, but all the visitors and new recruits and Villa's cadre did not know his/her story.

"HA!" Villa said, leaning forward, wide-eyed to stare at

Zamora closely, with exaggerated expressions and a jutted jaw as though he was trying to see past the thick make-up.

"Can you tell!?" he asked everyone. "Can you see dis?"

Villa looked at all their faces.

"Major Venzula? Can you see dis deception?"

Venzula stared at Zamora.

"General Fierro, can you see dis engano? De deception?"

He too studied Zamora.

"Perhaps…perhaps I am wrong? I am wrong, Miss Zamora? Perhaps we should see if I am wrong?"

Villa snapped his fingers at Venzula. On cue, Venzula stood up and stepped to the back of Zamora's chair. He grabbed Zamora's shoulders with great force and yanked the witch up. Zamora gyrated like a penned animal. Villa snapped his fingers at Fierro and the Butcher came close. He reached down and pulled up Zamora's long dress. Underwear was visible for those about the table tops nearby.

"Ladies underwear!" Villa declared with a raised hand. "Ahhh, so far, so good. Hey?"

Jefe shifted in his chair across the room and his hand inched down near his pistol, but Gunther saw this and slowly shook his head side-to-side. No.

Villa, like a vaudevillian comic moved his head to look at the faces at the big table.

"Let us see deeper into dis misterio?"

Fierro pulled the lace underwear down hoping to expose male genitalia. There was none!

Then Fierro stepped back and slapped the right cheek of Zamoras rear end. Hard. Zamora shook in sudden shock, legs spread and down dropped a cock and balls from a tucked position.

Villa clutched his heart with both hands and stumbled back, knocking his chair a few inches.

"It is TRUE!" Villa declared.

Zamora froze. People gasped.

"My amigo, Senor Gunther was correct then. And I am indebted to you sir, as dis...dis man-thing... had...had invited me to its bed tonight. Tonight! Oh my God, what a surprise dis would be for me." His face turned into a madman expression.

"How DARE you do dis to me."

Villa sat back down and sipped his lemonade.

"Perhaps....perhaps Mister Zamora would like to become a lady? A real lady? Right now?"

Venzula held Zamora tighter than ever.

"Take out your cuchillo, Fierro," Villa ordered.

And the Butcher pulled the long knife from his belt.

"Grab dee cock and dee balls," Villa said.

He did grab.

"You see, Mister Zamora, we can help you. We can fix you right now. We can make you the lady of your dreams, and after we remove you of your manliness, we can cut a big gash...up and down, Up and down. So...you can have such a nice, lady opening there too."

Dead silence. Everyone gaped at Villa. His face. His eyes. He tapped a finger on his glass.

"Oh but my apologies to my guests!" Villa said in a light tone. "My poor guests. My poor guests who must witness a man in a dress with a cock and balls....and den to have them removed right here, over such a dinner as dis. More wine, Senior Guillermo, for everyone, please." Villa slightly shook his head to Fierro, but Fierro had already started a small cut. Blood ran. He took the knife away, looking disappointed. The dress fell and Venzula let the man-woman go.

Zamora stood there. Free. Glaring at Villa.

Villa looked back, surprised.

"You can go, meeester Zamora," Villa said quietly.

"ALL of you....all of you..." Zamora said. She looked at Gunther, at Villa, at Venzula, at Fierro and the others at the table. "ALL OF YOU...are cursed. Cursed. In the name of Santa Muerta, I curse you. You will have THESE!" Zamora screamed, and reached into the purse hung from his shoulder. All the seated men touched the pistols in their holsters, but he pulled out a handful of beads. He tossed the necklaces one by one on the table.

"You need these rosary beads to pray for yourselves!"

The necklaces were long, each bead on the loop a green onyx-like stone. Each with the same stone medallion. One landed in front of Gunther, Jesus face up, as the medalling was onyx. Jesus on a onyx cross.

"DON'T touch them!" Chueng cried out. He sprang from his chair and ran closer to the table. "They are CURSED beads! Do NOT touch them in any way. Hercules!" he called for his bodyguard.

Hercules came to the table with a pool stick and started to hook the bead sets up.

Pancho's eyes grew wide as he looked around the table, for he was not without superstitions.

Zamora stormed out of the restaurant.

"Please, Senior Chueng, please sit by me for a moment," Villa said. Chueng got his chair and guitar and sat beside Villa. Hercules hooked the beads, careful to manipulate the stick and not to let the strands roll up and touch his hands.

"You," he said to Gunther, "have saved me from a most embarrassing moment tonight." Then he said to Chueng, "and YOU! You have saved me from a curse!"

Gunther remained expressionlesss, and Chueng looked down at the floor and shook his head.

"It is strange, is it not? Strange to hear de words 'Senor' and 'Chueng' together? One is a Spanish. One is a Chinese. Strange to put them together, I think. Senor Chueng. Senor Chueng. Hola! Hola! Guillermo! Bring Senor Chueng some wine, por favor."

The waiter did. The people at the long table began to talk amongst themselves, but Gunther stared at Villa. More wine was poured for the guests as they looked over their freshly arrived dinners. It was apparent that Zamora was a curse to this town, and scaring and hassling him was a relief. A justice.

A man in a three-piece suit, in front of another well-suited man approached Villa.

"Generalissimo, excuse me, but this is the man in charge of our local mercury mines. You've asked to meet him."

"Oh, oh yes," Villa said, motioning for the miner to step forward, "Sit! Sit."

"Hello, Generalissimo," the man said as he took an empty seat.

"Dis...dis is magic, you know. Dis substance of mercury. Yes?"

"Well yes. My name is Jose Delarosa."

"Jeees! I see that you are Mexican! Oh. Oh, I am so very proud," Villa said. "Proud that you own such a place in Texas."

"Oh sir, I am the general manager. Many men own the mine itself," he said.

"Yes, of course," Villa said.

Villa looked around at Gunther and all the faces near him. They followed Villa's moods and expressions like he was an orchestra leader.

"Still, it is a good job, huh?"

"Yes sir, it is."

"Do you have many Mexicans working in the mines?"

"Yes sir, and they are well paid too."

"Maravilloso!" Villa declared. "It is my dream you know, for all Mexicans to be...to be rich and happy."

"Si, Senor Generalissimo."

"Do you...do you have any...any Chinese in the mines?"

"No sir."

"Ahhhh. Good." Villa said as he turned and looked at Chueng with wide eyes. "Dis...dis mercury...it looks like...like the silver líquido dat we see...we see in the termómetro? Do you find it in underground, ahhhh, silver quinielas?"

"Oh no, sir. When we mine it, and it is very hard to find, mercury is rare. Although it is a naturally occurring, liquid substance, it is never found in pools. It only occurs as very small blobs on top of mercury ores such as, something the geologists call cinnabar..."

The translator translated.

"Cinna-bar," Villa repeated. Like...like in Americano... cinnamon."

"Cinnabar. The tiny blobs are lodged in small crevices or pores of cinnabar, or just stick to the host mineral. The blobs do not roll around or fall off, but stay attached in various positions."

The translator explained the terms. Villa's eyebrows shot up, and he looked around at everyone again, sharing the astonishment.

Jose tapped a finger on the table and reached into his jacket pocket. The quick movement was not unnoticed by the men standing around Villa and even...Gunther. Jose smiled and produced...a clear glass vial from inside his jacket. He took the cork top out and poured a little silver ball onto the table. It was obvious in a second that the ball was soft and fluid. In the other hand he held a business card and pushed the ball around a bit on the table, to the oohs and ahhs of the onlookers.

"Mercury," the miner said. "This is what you see in the thermometer."

"It is a bit of magic? Magic from the Rio Grande Valley, no? Yes?" Villa said.

"Yes, it is like magic," the miner said. "It has been very 'magical' for our city."

Villa reached out to the little ball. Gunther quickly dropped his palm on Villa's hand.

"I would not touch this, General," Gunther said.

"Ahh?" Villa said.

"No Generalissimo," the miner said. "It is not wise to touch it."

"Touch it? Like poison?"

"Yes," Gunther said.

"How is dis?"

"It...enters your body, like...like heat from the sun. It leaks in," Gunther tried to explain.

Villa's eyes passed from Gunther's to the miner.

"Si," the miner said.

"Then it is like de Rio Grande, black magic!" Villa declared.

The miner scooped the ball back into the vial with the card. Then sealed it with a cork. He handed the vial to Villa.

"Please...a gift," the miner said. "A gift if you promise not to open it and touch it."

"I will *not*!" Villa said, taking the gift with a big smile.

Gunther could not help but imagine that this sadistic bastard would someday make someone swallow the mysterious, silver ball.

"So, two times now you have saved me, Lt Gunther," Villa said to Gunther.

Gunther just smiled.

"Tell me Jose, since you have a big mining business here," Villa asked, "you must have a golf course here? Huh?"

"Ahhh, si. Si senor we do. The Mercury Golf Club. Yes," Jose said, with an inviting expression.

"Hahaaa, mercury! Of course."

"Would you like to play golf there, sir? As my guest?"

"As long as we don't play for money!" Villa proclaimed loudly.

All the people at the table laughed, which delighted Villa.

"And you see, sir, we have the manager of the golf course with us tonight."

Delarosa stood and shouted to a woman several tables away.

"April! April!" he shouted.

A woman from another table looked at him.

He waved his hand for her to come over. She got up.

"She is a female golf pro from Palm Springs, California. She manages the golf course here."

As she walked over she smiled, and Gunther took stock. She was a blonde, but not a natural one. She walked and looked like a silent film, movie star. Beautiful silver dress. Heels. Lots of makeup. About 40.

"Miss March, I would like to introduce to you our distinguished guest, Generalissimo Pancho Villa."

Gunther did the calendar math. Miss March. That meant her name was April March. Really?

"It is a pleasure, sir." She shook Villa's hand as he stood so fast, he almost knocked his chair over again.

"The General would like to play golf tomorrow."

"That would be wonderful," she said.

"You see I am just learning. I like this golf."

"When is a good time for you gentlemen?"

"Early tomorrow morning. I have mucho business the whole day. Siete?"

"Seven it is, sir."

"Should I pick you up somewhere?" Delarosa asked.

"No...no. No. Venzula will learn of This place, and he will take me there. I have no golf clothes, you know. None of thee clubs."

"This is no problem, sir," Miss April March said. "Well then, I will see you all tomorrow then."

As she turned, her eyes passed over Gunther. If she was intimidated by Villa, she did not let on. Her gaze lingered on Gunther for a long second. All the men at that end of the table watched her walk away.

"She is like de movie star, heh?" Villa said. "She is de real senorita."

The food was coming out for their end of the table.

Villa leaned back in his chair and looked at nearby Chueng, seated with his guitar. Villa asked Chueng, "You know, I love to see the beautiful homes, the casas of the Americans. The rich Americans. I read about them and I hear about them. I see de pictorials. Does Tremboro have such a place? A place of nice, big houses? I would love to see them."

"Si senor."

Gunther listened to this conversation.

"Si," Chueng continued. "There is a place to the north of town where many important people live. Important to the mining business..."

"Yes..."

"Important to government business..."

"Yes, de goberment...perhaps I will get someone to drive me by there to see their very nice Americano house. We can dream, you know? Is there, is there anyone here that lives there?"

"Most everyone here tonight lives there."

"Ahhhh," Villa said. He looked over the people with a different discerning look in his eye.

"You know...what were we saying un momento ago? Oh yes, de mines." Villa continued his conversation with Chueng, sounding less sing-songy and more serious. "You know that the Chinese...the Chinese in Mexico....a problemo," Villa said loud enough for all nearby to hear. "In Mexico, we have de mines in Sonora. Many Mexicans worked there. They have jobs. Poor jobs, but they have jobs. Then, then Senor Chueng, you see, de Chinese come. They come and they come and took these jobs from de Mexicans. For less monies. And, and my Mexicans are...so, so poor. Poor."

Villa, loud, was still really directing this to Chueng, but making a speech for all nearby to hear. Chueng waited in silence.

"One day...one day? I was near de mines. My men and I. I get all the Chinese together, as best I can, you know because it is hard to get so many people together. Six hundred of them. But all my men do this. Oh, my God, you know? And, I...kill them all," he said calmly. He sipped his drink.

"Not me. It is too much work for me. I mean, I have them killed because I myself cannot kill six hundred Chinese myself, you know. General Fierro and Major Venzula...they do all the work. The...killing work."

Chueng's eyes widened.

"Yes...and so, so I don't like the Chinese." Villa sipped again. "But you Senor, you have helped save me from a great curse tonight with this...this man-woman problemo. And from touching the black magic poison. And from touching the cursed beads. Muchos gracias. And you will helpa' me with many guns tomorrow."

"And you, Mister American." Villa looked at Gunther. "Ahhh the Americans. But you are German. I have a general from Germany, you know. His name is Velmer. He is a bery good man with a military mind. He was in de Prussian army. I pay him so much? He...he joins me. Much." Villa took a bite from a sopapilla.

"The Americans! I was once a great friend of the Americans. You gave me guns! You gave me trains! You gave me coal! You gave me supplies! You gave me money! Viva! Viva la Revolucion! But your President Wilson? Now? Now? Now this Wilson...he cuts me off like a dog. He no like me anymore."

Gunther nodded.

"Why?" Gunther asked.

"I don't know why? Maybe someday you can find out and you can tella' me! You are a military man, Senor Gunther."

"Was."

"Is. Was. I could pay you very much too."

Gunther half smiled. He too took a bite out of a sopapilla.

"How much?" Villa asked. "$100 a month. American money, not pesos."

"Let me think about," Gunther said, lying. Stalling.

"Well don't think too long because I tink I am leaving bery' soon."

Villa lightly slapped Chueng's shoulder with the back of his fingers. "It is too quiet! Please. Please sing a happy song so we can forget about a witch with a hidden cock, these beads of a curse, and a black magic silver ball of...of poison. Please!"

A tall, blond man wandered in, in a light-colored suit. As he approached the table, Villa called him over.

"Colonel Charming! Here. Sit here by us. Sit!"

The man's eyes cut to Gunther. His face expressionless. Gunther knew instantly this was not any such *real* Colonel Charming. This was in fact a British diplomat, George Hall whom he met in the Khyber Pass about eight years ago. But Gunther said nothing. He smiled the smile of a stranger. He had flashbacks of Afghanistan, of his near death and how George Hall took him to the best military hospital in India. He thought of their daily recovery walks, with him limping beside Hall on the pathways running beside of the Ganges River.

"Colonel Charming! Colonel is de retired British Military, this is Major Johann Gunther, retired US Army," Villa said. "Not the German Army!"

Gunther stood and reached across the table and shook the man's hand.

"Not retired. Just mustered out," Gunther corrected.

"I see. Wise choice, old chap. Such saves time in ones life. And ones life at times."

"Colonel Charming," Villa continued, "has joined our cause. I am trying to get Major Gunther to join our little cause too."

The cook brought a plate of food to Charming as the Brit swept open the napkin across his lap.

"Tell me, Major Johann Gunther, retired..." Charming said.

"Mustard out..." reminded Gunther.

"Do you want mustard?" Villa asked, then shouted for Guillermo, "Mustard!"

"Yes...mustard out..." Charming corrected himself. "Do you like Mexican food?"

"Yes, very much."

"Good, because if you do join our...little...cause here, there will be much Mexican food. I believe the word is...mucho."

"Ahhhhhahahah," Villa burst out in laughter, but still chewing.

Gunther and this "Charming" stared at each other for a moment, and Gunther wondered just how a frightened diplomat named George Hall, he'd met once in Afghanistan, was now sitting before him some eight years later, pretending to be a retired soldier at the table of a Mexican madman, general.

"Mustard, senor?" Guillermo said, holding a small plate of the brown stuff before Gunther.

"Ah...yeah. Sure," Gunther said with a smile. "Just...just put it right down there."

After eating, the local guests - international soldiers, cowboys and some timid citizens wandered around the room, many with a cigar in one hand and a glass of tequila in the other, Gunther positioned himself by a front row of windows overlooking the street. As expected, Colonel Charming eventually joined him. They stared out on the street as they spoke quietly.

"Hello, Johann."

"Hello, George."

"I see you've healed well from all your Afghan wounds," the Brit said.

"I have. Thanks to you. How are you?"

"I am fine. Busy."

"I see you are busy," Gunther said. "Busy being someone else."

George Hall sipped his drink and took a casual look around.

"After we last met, I left the diplomatic core for British Intelligence. As you might recall from our last conversation in India, you inspired me to a higher service."

"I do recall that."

Hall turned with his back to the windows so he could watch the room.

"I have been on several assignments, and this is one of them."

"Villa," Gunther said.

"Yes. There is a war coming, Johann. A very big war. Started by your homeland, Germany. It simply must involve the United States, and it will involve Mexico."

"Mexico?"

"There are already plans underway. Villa's already got a bloody German on his staff. Manipulating him. Turning Villa against the US."

"Wilson doesn't seem to be helping. Villa has asked me to join him also," Gunther said.

Hall smiled and waved at someone over Gunther's shoulder.

"What do you do for Villa?" Gunther asked.

"We plan wars. We plan attacks. He does not listen and mad rushes every place like a tidal wave. He is a madman," Hall-Charming said.

"Are you there...present...for the war crimes. The killing and torture?" Gunther asked.

"Sometimes, yes."

"What will you do if there is a European war?" Gunther asked.

"I don't know. Spying I presume. If it even happens. I will have to wait and see, but I hope nothing."

"Nothing?"

"Nothing." Hall-Charming said

"Here's to nothing," Gunther said.

They touched whiskey glasses and smiled.

"Hmmmm. There is something you can do for me, old chap," Hall whispered.

Gunther's head slightly nodded up and down. He added a slight sigh, not in an agreement but more of a *here it comes,* anticipatory manner. His eyes roamed the street outside.

"I need help," Hall said. "I need to reach the London Embassy in Washington with a report."

A gunshot blasted off, followed by a howl behind them. A cowboy fired his handgun into the ceiling, for some reason. Men laughed. Villa laughed. Neither Gunther nor Hall jumped. Gunther noted Hall's calm. Not the quaking, George Hall he remembered back in the Khyber Pass. A waiter ran up to the cowboy to stop him from shooting again. This made Gunther think of the missing, local Marshal Preston Heston. Where was he this night?

"I have to report in," Hall continued. "Developments."

"Developments," Gunther repeated in his own whisper.

"We are all over the countryside. I never get a chance to contact anyone, if even by mail. Weeks go by. If I passed you a report, just a few pages, you could get it to an American post office and send it to our embassy in Washington DC. I must check in with them."

"There's a post office here in town."

"I can't get to it, Gunth. I can't get free to get to it. I am constantly in the company of these scoundrels. I have one bodyguard, and I don't know if he's a bloody spy or a life saver. And I can't use such a small post office like this one. Addressed to...the embassy? Busy bodies everywhere. It needs to go out from a big post office. Such as...such as San Antonio. You could mail it. Are you leaving on a train for San Antonio?"

"Yes."

"When?"

"Hopefully tomorrow. Worse...the day after tomorrow."

"Good."

"We want to buy some guns for a security job first thing in the morning and then get the hell out of here," Gunther said.

"Ohhh dear chap, you shan't be buying any guns here. Villa will take all the guns. Tomorrow."

"I was...afraid of that. The train leaves tomorrow. I'll get over to the gun store first thing in the morning and get some guns."

"Good idea. He does sleep late. Usually. So you have a chance. Leave with my letter tomorrow. Oh yes, and the guns? He won't be buying them. He'll just take them. No buying."

"I just heard he is playing golf in the morning."

"Probably. He's a golfer of late," Hall/Charming said.

"How will you get it to me?" Gunther asked.

"Where are you staying?"

"Right there across the street. La Contessa. I'll be sitting out on the porch tonight."

Hall turned toward the windows. He saw the front porch.

"Okay. Do sit outside tonight," Hall said. He looked pensively down to the floor, then said, "Could you add your observations also?"

Gunther winced a bit. "My...."

"Your trained observations. Be candid. Write your name and say that you know me from Afghanistan. Your opinions will be highly regarded. Trust me."

"Ohhhh-okay."

Hall smiled broadly, as if a joke passed between them.

"Don't get caught with it," he whispered, "as they will hang us upside down and skin...us...alive. Very slowly."

Hall walked off toward Villa and his cluster of men. Gunther watched him for a few seconds. He remained at the window.

"Who might you be?" a female voice asked from his left.

He turned. It was Miss April March.

She held a champaigne glass in her black, gloved hand.

He nodded, "Ma'am. Name's Gunther. Johann Gunther."

"From?"

"Lately...Ft Worth."

"Lately?"

"Well, originally Germany," Gunther said for the second time that night.

"I fail to detect an accent," she said.

"I fail to have one. Been here a long time."

"You are not here to join this motley cast?"

"No ma'am, just more or less, passing through."

"You sat by Villa like his right hand man."

"I am...prior military, and he wants me to join his shindig, thus the close seat, but I shall pass."

"A wise man."

They looked at each other just a bit too long, forgetting the social graces of a proper time to stare. She was a bit close, and he took in her whole face, hair and neck, almost breathing her in.

She raised her empty hand, "Miss April March."

"Miss March," he shook her hand. "A very timely name."

She sipped.

"While you seem *very* much in order," Gunther said, trying hard to keep his eyes on her eyes and not look below, "your name isn't quite in order, shouldn't it be Miss March first, then April?"

"Perhaps, but I'm still very much in the category of spring," she said.

"That you are. I like that category. Speaking of names, did you know that Pancho Villa's real name is not Pancho Villa?"

"No!"

"His real name is José Doroteo Arango Arámbula. The original Pancho Villa was a somewhat famous Mexican bandit from many years ago. José stole the name."

"I didn't know," she said.

"We could be looking at someone who calls himself Robin Hood."

"Robin who?"

"But, I am here for a day or two," Gunther said, changing the subject. "How...how did you end up here in Tremboro, Texas?" Gunther asked.

"Golf. Golfing. I have won some tours on a women's circuit. I got a divorce...he was my husband and my manager and a damn good caddy too, shame, and well...I needed a change."

"Yes. A change."

"And I read in the *San Diego Times*, that the mining company out here needed a golf pro to run their new establishment. The course is very nice. The salary very nice."

"I see. Will you...ever...play again?" he asked as he sipped his whiskey.

She almost laughed. "I really don't know. Depends on the game, I guess."

He nodded.

"Maybe you just need to find that right caddy," he said.

"Maybe. Do you play golf?" she asked.

"Not yet. I...."

"April!" came a male voice from behind.

"Oh, I have to go," she said. "My, ah, my... friend... tonight...we are marching in the Day of the Dead Parade."

"Well, I hope to see you parade right by. Where are you parading by?"

"Right outside. This avenue. But you won't recognize me. I'll be wearing a skeleton mask."

"Oh, I always recognize when spring is in the air. It was nice to meet you, Miss March."

"Oh, you can call me April, doll. Nice to meet you too."

As she left, Gunther crossed the crowded room to Jefe, still seated with Calabash. Gunther motioned his head for Jefe to join him near the front doors where they could talk in private. Jefe, holding a coffee mug of water, as he did not drink alcohol either, met Gunther by the entrance.

"Do you remember...remember when I was healing up in India at that British hospital?"

"Yes, of course."

"The Brit who visited me every day and brought me Latissimo's sword?"

"Yes, of course. Yes," Jefe said.

"That Brit right there? That Brit? Is *that* man."

Jefe's eyes widened incredulously. He half smiled in disbelief.

"Wha....noooo..."

"Wha...yes. He is now with British Intelligence and he is pretending to be a retired Royal officer. To spy on Villa."

Jefe slowly turned and casually scanned the room, making a quick study of the Brit.

"He's asked me to smuggle a report out for him," Gunther said.

"Allah be praised," Jefe said in depression. "We...we have to get out of here as soon as possible. This is turning into a Shakespeare play. One of his more bloody ones. Crazy things are happening."

"Methinks so too, amigo."

The cowboys got a little rowdy. The soldados got drunk. The women got nervous. Gunther walked to a table to put his empty glass down. He took a quick look around before leaving and spotted yet another man in the room who was also a fake, another spy, someone pretending to be someone else. Should he introduce the two spies to each other? Too risky? Too deadly?

The corpulent man shouted, "The parade will begin in one hour! All those in the parade must prepare."

Chapter 5: By the Neck of the Black Horse
August 1924, Omaha, Nebraska

"I thought the whole war was gonna' start off right there on the street, right after dinner. Gunther started mixing it up with Venzula over Venzula's horse," Calabash told the officers.

"What happened?" General Pershing asked.

"Venzula was torturing his horse with a knife. He called it training his horse. And, Gunther loves horses. So..."

****

October 1915, Tremboro, Texas

The parade. Soon to start.

Gunther, Jefe and Calabash left the restaurant, alongside several of Villa's men and some local citizens. Some were going to watch the parade. Some, were in the parade. Gunther stepped off to the side, and pulled out a cigar and matches from his jacket pocket. He flicked the front of his hat brim, and the Stetson jumped up an inch off his brow. Jefe and Calabash walked with him.

A horse suddenly cried out and the sound caught the men's attention. The steed shuffled a bit amongst the nearby Mexicans and their horses. Major Venzula stood by the nervous black horse as he drew a knife back from the horse's neck, wiped the knife tip on the mane and returned it to his belt sheath.

Gunther started walking back to the group. "Did he just cut that horse?"

"Don't," Jefe said.

Gunther ignored him.

"Allah be with us," Jefe muttered and stepped off to the right to get a better view from the street. Jefe, always the smartest, best cover man, knew when there would be trouble and always knew where to position himself to back up his old friend.

Gunther walked up to Venzula and the horse, brushing past several soldiers. He saw many vertical scars on the black horse's neck and now this new, long, thin, fresh, red blood line.

"Beautiful horse," Gunther said, interrupting Venzula's conversation with a few of his men.

"He is," Venzula said, instinctively knowing why Gunther was suddenly there, and Venzula smiled with the hope for deadly trouble with the Americano. "You did not wait for my escort at your hotel."

"I got hungry."

"Dis could be a sign of disrespect."

"Where did he get all of these?" Gunther asked, pointing to the scars and new blood on the horse's neck.

"Every day or so, amigo, I cut a new, thin line on de horse's neck."

"You do?"

"I do."

"What for?"

"To...to make sure he understands who is dee boss, huh? He is after all, my animal. To do with as I wish. I make sure he sees me when I do dis. Eyes to eyes. I know just how much of the tip of the knife to touch the cuello, very lightly. The horse will...how you say...ahhh...rebuild...remake...the blood. Juzz' a little cut. And de lesson will begin again tomorrow." Venzula smiled, but warily. One of the ragged revolutionaries smiled beside him. They could sense bad trouble.

"I see," Gunther said. "So this...this is a horse training idea?"

"Si."

Gunther saw the rash of short scars down either side of the horse's barrel too as he walked around it. Also new slices, fresh from today. He looked down to see Venzula's sharp looking spurs.

"What's the horse's name?" Gunther asked.

"Funny you should ask dis, senor...with de witch Zamora here tonight, and de churches and de witches in did village, but de horse's name is Black Magic."

"Black...Magic...huh. Yeah, that is funny. We say in English, a...coincidence."

"Yes...dee coincidencia."

They stood still and quiet for a few seconds.

"The Generalissimo tells me dat you are thinking about joining our ranks. Dat you were once an important American soldier."

"I am thinking about it."

"Because..." he stoked his moustache. "If you were not thinking about it, I would be very concerned about you walking up to me like dis and asking about how I train my horse."

Gunther nodded.

"Because I could...just shoot you for...for asking...you know...about my particular methods in horse training. It is none of your business."

Gunther smiled. "Horse...training," he said.

Venzula smiled.

"What a waste that would be," Gunther said quitely. "What a waste for the Revolution. Because, I would shoot you back." Gunther rolled his cigar in his mouth.

Venzula glanced toward the street and spotted Jefe off to his side, staring at them intently. Jefe was not smiling, either.

"And then," Gunther continued, "then we would *both* be dead, and who would be left to care about this horse? And its training? And to help in the Revolution? And...and this ain't Mexico, amigo."

"So, you think you are bery fast?" Venzula asked.

"Oh no, no...not fast. Not too fast." Gunther said with a fake chuckle. "But I have been shot before. In Cuba. In the Philippines. In Arkansas. Oklahoma." He stroked the horse's neck. "In Texas. And every time? I killed the person who shot me."

"Every time," Venzula repeated.

"Eeeevery single time. Not because I am so fast. I just get very angry with pain. Have you ever been shot, Senor Venzula?"

"No. No I have not. I have shot many people..."

"So I hear..."

"...but I have never been shot."

"Perhaps *you* are very fast then," Gunther said. "Or very clever."

"Perhaps."

"Is this horse for sale?" Gunther asked, wandering from the face-to-face confrontation to look the horse over again.

"Hmmm, I don't know," Venzula said. "How much?"

"Twenty dollars?"

"Twenty dollars! You have $20?" Venzula's eyes wandered all over Gunther's jacket. "On you?"

"Somewhere."

"Perhaps, I should just shoot you and take dis money. HA!"

Gunther just smiled and released a single laugh. "Then you would have the problem again of being alive to spend it."

"For $20 American dollars, I would sell dis horse."

Gunther pulled out some money from a pants pocket, counted off $20 in bills and started to hand them to Venzula, then brought his fingers with the money back.

"The tack too? The saddle and everything too for an extra $5? They are very nice."

"For $25 dollars? HA! Of course."

He gave Venzula the money. He took the reins and walked off with the horse.

Venzula laughed.

"I will just get another horse," he said to Gunther's back.

Gunther said nothing.

"You...you cannot save all my horses," Venzula said a little louder as Gunther and Black Magic walked off.

"But, I can save this one," Gunther said, not turning around.

Venzula gave Jefe a nasty sneer. Jefe stood still until Gunther got far enough away. The soldiers mounted their horses. Venzula told one man to get off his horse, and Venzula climbed on it. The soldier would walk. They rode off.

Gunther passed Jefe, his new horse in tow. Calabash watched the whole encounter from afar. He'd quickly started sweating.

"You are a crazy man," Jefe growled, shaking his head as Gunther and the horse walked by. Jefe saw the blood line scars on the horse's neck, up close.

"Yeah. Crazy for the horses," Gunther said.

Chapter 6: Air of the Warlock
September 1924, Tremboro, Texas

"Mr Clark, you are one of the few people we can find that actually saw Pancho Villa interact with Johann Gunther," General Pershing said. "I know it was many years ago, but do you remember that dinner?"

Pershing and Lt Hawes were in the Rotunda restaurant in Tremboro, Texas. Steven F. Clark was still the owner of the eatery.

"I will never forget it," Clark said. "Who can forget feeding Pancho Villa? Who can forget what he and his men did to Tremboro?"

"How would you describe the dinner? How did they act? Was there any trouble, any animosity you could detect between them?"

"None."

"None at all?"

"No. At one point Villa reached out to touch the sample of mercury the mining manager had laid on the table, and Gunther lunged out and stopped him. They were friendly. It looked to me that Villa liked Gunther very much. Then, the little war in our city came."

****

October 1915, Tremboro, Texas

From prior trips to Tremboro, Gunther knew right where the Harley Benz Car and Horse Stable was. Not too far to walk. He led the horse down a few side streets. Then he tied Black Magic up to a rail outside and walked into the car showroom, eyeing the four automobiles as he approached the counter.

"Peter, you are still here?" Gunther said, somewhat sarcastically.

"Where else can I go?"

Gunther smiled at him. "I would suggest Lake Tahoe but Tremboro is pretty this time of year."

"Pretty?" Peter said. "It looks like a fire crawled through. Colorful, yes, in the spring. The wild flowers. Looks like Ireland. Wait a few weeks. It'll all be on fire. Where's yer shadow?"

"Jefe's back at the hotel. Got one horse here."

"One?"

"Came in on the train and I just bought this horse?"

"From who?"

"From the revolutionaries."

"From those crazy-ass Mexicans?"

"Yup."

"I ain't seen much good horse flesh from any of them."

"This one is from an officer."

"Oh. How many nights, sir?"

"Don't know for sure. Two for starters?"

"Okey-dokey. Geeet' around back and our boy with catch up with ya. He's eatin' a plate of catfish and turnips right now, and we can't tear him away from that. I'll get him out there."

"Tell em to finish first." He put a dime on the counter.

"No hurry."

Gunther looked at the autos in the showroom.

"How's the car business going?" Gunther asked.

"It's going. Mining people buy em. Mayor. Golf club people. It's going. There's a decent dirt road now from here to San Antonio. They have paved some of it. The county will get around to paving the whole thing. That'll help sales. I sell about...one, two a month. People order them from catalogs and picture ads. I get em in from San Antoine pretty quick."

"Hey, ever rent any of these cars?" Gunther asked while walking out.

"Rent em'? What kind a crazy-ass idea is that?"

Gunther smirked and walked Black Magic around the side of the brick showroom and into one of the empty stalls in the dimly lit stable. He picked a stall under a good light bulb, and under the bare bulb he examined the thin slices on the horse's neck and spur wounds on the body. There were numerous scars. A few slices with the scabs and the new dark red one from tonight."

"You!" came a voice from a dark corner.

"Hello Celesta," Gunther said without turning. "I'd know your 'you' anywhere. What are you doing here?" he asked.

"Theez horse is beautiful," she said.

"Yes."

"Theez horse is more than beautiful," she said. She walked up to it and began rubbing her grimy palms on the horse. In the bare electric light bulb, he could see she was in a torn, flannel shirt and muddy black skirt. Barefoot.

"Watch out for his neck. That sick idiot has been cutting on it."

"Venzula," she said.

"Yeah."

Gunther rested his arm on a stall post and asked again,

"What are you doing back here in a barn?"

Celesta rounded the horse and ran her hands all over the metal studs of the elaborate saddle.

"To tell you theez. Pancho Villa has 34 men in a camp outzide de town. He has 12 men with him in dee town. He will buy another 17 new men."

Gunther nodded and said, "I didn't know about the men in the camp."

She put her palms on her bald head and sucked in a lot of air. Frustration? Headache?

"How do you know this?" he asked.

"I have seen de camp. I go there. I prayed for dem in de camp. I counted de men here with Villa. I pray for dem. I have seen all de new men come for jobs for de Revolution."

"Have you prayed for the new men, too?"

"Not yet."

She walked up to him. Too close. He could smell her.

"Dis is de horse of Venzula."

Gunther nodded.

"And there was a problem with dis horse and Venzula. Dey did not match. Dis black horse is a good horse. It has good feelings for de world. Venzula, like Zamora, is bad. When dey rode by me, there was a problem in the air. And de horse called out to me."

Gunther half smiled at her.

"Is he talking to you now?" Gunther asked, stepping away from her. "Cause if he is, he's saying you need a good, hot bath."

"No need. And you? You also smelled the bad air of Venzula and felt this horse's pain. Because of the same bad air, you saved him. He called out to you didn't he? Tonight? He knew to send you a message for help."

"You know Celesta, you people, you...seers, you fortune tellers,have a way of taking the obvious, painting over it with odd poetry, and making it sound like magic."

"Dat what you think?"

"That's what I think," Gunther said.

"Den....den you should ask Father Columbus about his right hand."

"The Catholic priest?" Gunther asked.

"Si. I put a curse on his right hand."

"His right hand?"

"Si. You..." she stepped back and glared at Gunther. "He

was too busy in love with his right hand. You...senor, You are busy in love with Africa."

"Af...rica?" he said with a quizzical expression.

"You are in love with Africa. Someone from Africa."

Gunther shook his head. He put his hat on the stable post and started to unbuckle the saddle.

"Africa is still alive," she said in almost a low growl.

"Africa is dead," Gunther said quickly, surprising himself with such a quick answer, or for answering at all.

"She will come to you."

He stopped and looked at her, "Why are you telling me this?"

"She will come to you, someday."

Unsteady with this news, this advice, he sneered a bit and removed the saddle.

"You still think I am painting over a picture with words of magic poetry?" she asked.

Gunther stopped and stared at her.

"Dis horse has magic and you have magic, senor, magic in your air. You are like a warlock, senor. You always have been. Dere is..." she waved her hands in the air around him, "an air about you of de warlock."

He shook his head.

"I can tell you more?" she said.

"You can, huh?"

"But, first. First, you must make love to me," she said.

Gunther's eyebrows shot up, and he looked at her. She sat back on a small square bail of hay. She spread her legs wide, pulled up her skirt and rubbed her palms on the insides of her thighs.

Gunther watched her hands. Hands on horse. Hands on bald head. Now hands on thighs.

"And why's that?"

"I need your magic in me to read your magic. And give you more power. Is simple."

"Lady...that ain't gonna happen." He went back to work, undoing the halter and reins.

"Come into me."

"I gotta tell ya, this is a new line of seduction I've never heard before, Celesta."

"Don't you want to know what will happen to you? Your love of Africa? Do you want to know what will happen to dis town tomorrow?"

"What will happen to this town tomorrow?"

She squeezed her thighs with her hands. Her eyebrows raised and she began to stroke her crotch.

"You know...a nun wouldn't cut a deal like that," Gunther said.

"I am not a nun."

"Yeah. Aren't you supposed to be the *good* witch?"

"I am a witch, and I need my magic pieces to make my witch magic. And, I will bring you magic too."

"And, that's another paint job," Gunther said.

He turned on a spicket from the wall, grabbed the hose and filled a metal bucket of water. Then he ran some of the water on the horse's cut neck.

"Sorry! Sorry sir!" said a teenage stable boy who skipped into sight. "I was eating."

Celesta looked at the boy and stood, the hemline dropping past her knees. She approached Gunther, with a serious and frightening face and said in whisper, "Now I send you a message. Tomorrow, Villa will burn dis city."

He stopped watering.

"You hear something?"

"I know something."

"How?"

"I smell it. I see it in the air. It is a cloud among all his men. Villa will destroy dis city. Dat is why I tried to stop you at de train station."

She backed away from him, nodding her head up and down.

"I have blessed your horse," she said calmly.

She left him standing there with the watering hose in his hand.

Chapter 7: The Devil Wears a Goatee
August 1924, Omaha, Nebraska

Calabash continued with his recollections, "We left the restaurant and Jefe and I grabbed some rockers in front of our hotel. On the porch. There was a little patio area out front. Gunther had walked off with his new horse without any trouble from Venzula. And...whew! He left for a local barn er somethin'. Then he showed up again and sat down next to us. He told us he'd met the bald witch at the barn."

"Did it seem to you that Venzula would become Gunther's enemy over this horse?" General Pershing asked.

"To me? Hell yeah. They wuz' breathin' fire nose to nose. To me they damn near killed each other there on the street. But Jefe, that sly, slinky devil, he wormed his way around them. He stood there like a rattler about to strike. Lookin back, knowin' what I know now? If something would have happened, I have no doubt in my ever-lovin' mind Jefe would a killed about six of em. And missed all the horses to boot. But, the secret? Their secret? And I knew this that night. Them two? They would die if they had to. Right there. That night. Over just that horse."

Pershing stared at Calabash. He pursed his lips and nodded his head.

"That sudden. Maybe you know that secret," Calabash said. "Maybe it's an army-man secret? But those two would have died that night and them others? Not. They didn't wanna. They didn't wanna die. At least not that night. Right then. That is the secret. That is what kept them alive. Willing to die kept them alive.

Next though, I saw the damndest duel I've ever seen right out there on the street!"

****

October 1915, Tremboro, Texas

Gunther walked back to the main street and the hotel. He tried to shake his head free of the witch's talk. There was considerable activity on the avenue. Many of Villa's men were gone. Only a few of the new mercenary, recruits lingered in front of the Rotunda.

Jefe and Calabash were seated in rocking chairs in front of the hotel, in the middle of a mild breeze. Gunther sat in a rocker too and immediately started rocking.

"What cha drinking?" he asked them.

"China tea," Jefe said.

"Bourbon," Calabash said. "Clerk said the bar is open for another hour or two."

"As I recall, the coffee here is real good," Gunther said. "Is Randy still around?"

Calabash was in the best position to look through the open front doors.

"There's the young feller now, HEY!" Calabash called in.

Rock Candy Randy came out.

"How's about a black coffee, Randy? You got any made fresh?" Gunther asked.

"We can make ya some fresh."

"Well, don't make a whole new pot just for me."

"We make it, Nister Nunther. You...you destherve good coffee."

"Okay then. Where are our boys?" Gunther asked Jefe.

"They are in their room, playing a board game," Jefe said.

Gunther laid his hat on a table by the front wall and ran a hand through his blond hair.

"Celesta said," Gunther piped up, "that Villa and his men will destroy this town tomorrow."

"Cel...esta?" Jefe said.

"She was waiting for me in the stable."

Jefe shook his head with the news. "How did she know you would be there?"

"Who knows?"

"She thinks that Villa and just these 15 - 20 men will lay waste to this village?" Jefe asked.

"Oh, she says there's more men. She says there are about 30 men or so camped on the outskirts of town."

"That's about 50 men all together," Jefe said.

"She may have heard something. She's been out to their camp 'praying' for the men."

"Praying. Oh," Jefe said in disgust. "She preys with that wet nasty thing between her legs."

"You know how these people work. They hear something, then they claim they predict the future," Gunther said.

"Magic!" Calabash said. "Here's to it! And to the wet thing betwixt a lady's legs." He raised his glass of bourbon, and took a swig. "Nasty!" he said with a grin.

"Yeah, I think she was going to rape me until the stable boy walked in," Gunther said, sipping the coffee.

Jefe shook his head, "She is a dirty creature," Jefe warned. "You stay away from her. You will have a disease that will destroy your life. One such disease and you will never marry a decent woman. And such a disease will kill your babies." Jefe, ever worried about Gunther's consorts, pointed a finger at him and grimaced. "*She's* a dirty dish rag."

"I told her that was not going to happen," Gunther admitted.

Jefe shifted in his chair and took a sip of his tea.

"Willin, are you now part of that 50 men?" Gunther asked.

"I...haven't even been interviewed yet, Gunth. Yet to be hired for Villa's American Legion," Calabash said. "Tomorrow."

"Villa's...American...Legion. That what they call it?" Gunther asked.

"We report to the restaurant again at 8 a.m."

"To do what? Be interviewed?"

"Uh-huh."

"How much they paying ya?"

"I hear 10 dollars and 50 cents a month."

"Hmmm."

"Hmmm, what? Plus all the food, clothes and a horse. All that, yeah. They will offer you more Gunth, seeing on how you were an officer and Villa has taken a shine to ya."

Randy showed up with a mug of coffee for Gunther, handed it off and left.

"Let him think that for as long as possible. But looky here, Jefe and I need to hire some men to protect the Whittle family and ranch near Brownsville. $10 a month. With room and board. Meals. Any horse free to use. It won't be no sorry pony like some of these guys are riding."

"How long's awhile?" Calabash asked.

"A mite longer than you being killed next Wednesday in a war started by the whims of a pack of idiots!" Gunther said. "You know how Villa attacks forts and cities?"

"Nope."

"He just charges them. All at once. Everyone. Races up to and into the enemy with no other plan. It either works, or it don't. He has military advisors but he ignores them and still does this mad rush."

"So...you...asking?" Calabash said.

"Yup, right now. Right here. Better then running ragged over the Sierra Madre, shot at by the Federales, or...or tortured to death cause you looked cross-eyed at Fierro or Venzula."

Calabash sipped his bourbon. His lower lip protruded, and his tongue bounced up and down making a wet, clicking noise.

"That's the sound of you thinkin', I reckon? The job starts now and involves having to take care of those boys too," Gunther said.

"Okay," Calabash said. "You are right. This is crazy. Crazy people. They were about to cut somebody's dick off in public. At least I'd still be in Texas and not over the border. Here's to America."

"You hear much talk from these other men?" Gunther asked.

"Yeah."

"Where they from?"

"Most is from US of A. But one is from Greece. One from Spain. One from Sweden."

"One of them...one of those boys, is a Texas Ranger," Gunther said quitely and with a small smile, then a big sip of coffee.

"Huh?" Calabash said.

"Must be the same beans as last time," Gunther said, "Dang business! This is a good cup of coffee. The feller on the train with the big-ass whip wrapped up on his belt? Army hat? The suspenders with the magazine carriers sewed on them? The checkered tie?"

"Yeah?" Calabash said. "Yeah."

"Smoking a pipe? About 40 years old?"

"Yeah!"

This also intrigued Jefe. He folded his arm across his chest and glared at Gunther.

"He is, or was, a Texas Ranger," Gunther said.

"He quit the Rangers to do this?" Calabash asked with a raised eyebrow.

"I'll bet not. I'll bet, I'll just betcha, he is a spy for them. We recognized each other on the train. He ever so slightly shook his head 'no' to me before I spoke to him. I think he is down here as a spy. He's a ranger from the Dallas company."

"What's his name? You know?" Jefe asked.

"Bullwhip Pierce. Bullwhip being a nickname. Don't know his real first name. That's all I know." Gunther turned to Jefe. "He and another Ranger, Frank Hamer, came to talk to me about Chester Winch years ago."

Jefe nodded.

"Whose Chester Winch?" Calabash asked.

Gunther sipped his coffee again, then said, "A very corrupt ranger in Ft Worth. One might say, he is my arch enemy."

"Like Napoleon and Waterloo?" Calabash said.

"Well..." Gunther smiled. "Wellington. Waterloo is a place."

"Yeah! Waterlog. That's it. What a day," Calabash said. "My head will explode like die-no-mite."

The three men sat in silence for a moment, watching the locals and "invader-tourists" linger about and walk the streets.

"You know," Jefe spoke up, "when Venzula leaves, he'll steal that horse back."

Gunther nodded.

"What will you do?" Jefe asked.

"I'll see when it happens."

"You'll see when it happens," Jefe repeated, shaking his head.

A good breeze wafted through to everyone's delight.

The Revolution candidates dispersed from the streets, heading back to other bars or their hotels. The bullwhip man in question, left the group and wandered away from the restaurant, when,

"Hey, Latigo! Latigo hombre!" one of the soldados shouted out.

The man with the whip stopped. He didn't turn around. He knew latigo translated to whip in Spanish.

"You like your whip, senor?" the man said.

He turned, "Yes, I do." The whip man eyed him up and down. The Latin was about 40 years old, thin, dressed in tight clothes. He had a flat brim, black hat pushed back on his head. He burnished a goatee and long black hair.

"What do you do wit dat whip?"

"I control horses. Buffalo. Cattle. Kill snakes..."

"KILL SNAKES!" the Latin said in amazement, but the emotion seemed fake.

"Yes."

Some of Villa's men and some recruits stood and watched.

"You...you hurt these animals?"

"Noooo, not my intention to hurt God's creatures. I just remind them I am there. And remind them to go elsewhere."

"Remind...si, senor. I am from...south of here. You heard of Brazil?"

"Yes."

"I am not from Brazil. But near there. We have...the bola." He undid a long rope from around his waist from his gun belt. Everyone watched him. Freed from his torso, the men could see a single length of rope, which branched off to the short lengths of rope, and three palm-sized, round ball-shaped stones at the end of each line.

He started to swing the contraption over his head, and the others grunted and bolted away from him, as the bola whistled in the wind.

"Can you make such a noise with your whip?"

"Just a crack like thunder."

"Can you hit small things with your whip?"

"Yes."

"Javier," the man called out. "Two bottles, eh?"

A thin man in a maroon sombrero grimaced, shook his head at being summoned in such a manner, but walked into the restaurant and emerged with two bottles of Montejo.

"Dey are full, yes?"

"Si," the man with the maroon sombrero said.

"Put dem on de rail."

With a reluctant shuffle, the man with the maroon sombrero set the bottles on the flat rail of the sidewalk.

"Set dem far apart, Javier."

He did.

"Can you break a bottle, Latigo?"

"This is the man of which you speak," Jefe whispered to Gunther.

"Yes," Gunther said.

The whip man unhooked his tool from his belt, exposing what looked like a twisted horseshoe sewn into his gun belt for a holster as a whip carrier. He rolled the whip out, snaked it side to side, looking at it like it was a pet rattler, then he looked up at the bottles. He reared back and threw his arm forward with a sudden controlled retraction at the end of the move. In a sound almost like a bullet blast, a crack out of thin air, the whip's tip hit the bottle, shattering the glass, and de-ported the beer like a small explosion.

"That's slicker than prairie dog shit," Calabash whispered, his jaw dropped.

The Latino with the bolo applauded. There were oohs and aahs from the onlookers. Some applause too.

"Muy bueno, Latigo," he said.

He stepped further back, swung his rocks again and let go. It was hard to discern what happened, like trying to see a wasp in a horde attack. One, two or all three stones hit the bottle, raking it off the rail and smashing it open. They hit the wooden wall of the restaurant and dropped.

More oohs and aahs.

"Very nice, sir," the whip man said. "But as you can see...I still have my whip and you have thrown away your bola."

"Can you catch someone? Can you stop someone with your whip?" the Latino asked.

"If he doesn't get too far."

"Javier!" the bola man called out as he retrieved his weapon from the sidewalk.

"Qué?" The man in the maroon sombrero said, annoyed. Frustrated. It was becoming apparent to the onlookers that Javier was the runt of the group.

"Javier. Run. Run up the avenida."

"Ohhh...oh no," Javier groaned.

"Go on, amigo," the bola man said, wrapping his bola on his belt.

Javier sheepishly walked to the middle of the street. He took a deep breath, sighed, and dashed up the avenue.

The man pulled the weapon from his belt, twirled it and flung at Javier. The stones and the rope wrapped Javier's legs together. He fell face first to the paved street, his maroon hat flying off and tumbling down the roadway.

More clapping. More gasps from Latinos and Americans alike.

Calabash was speechless. Gunther smiled. Jefe was nervous that this was going to get worse.

"Can your whip do this senor?"

"Yes," the whip man said.

Javier sheepishly untangled himself, cursing and moaning quietly in Spanish. His face had a big red rash from the road. He picked himself up, unwrapped his legs and walked back to the man, handing him the bola.

"Uno mas, amigo!" the bola man called out.

"Ay, Chihuahua!" Javier cried out. He limped back to his starting place.

The whip man sizzled his whip back and forth on the ground.

"Noooooo, no, senor," the bola man said. "From de hip. From de belt. Like me."

The whipster made that same undefined face. He rolled his whip a few times around the holster-hook-shoe-horn on his belt.

"GO!" the whip man yelled, and Javier took off. He unrolled the whip and with a special light snapping flick, fired his flexible weapon upon Javier just before the Mexican got a step too far. The whip caught the ankle, and Javier plummeted again. Grunting again. Hat flying again. Poor Javier fell, this time split-legged in almost a gawky cartwheel as the whip peeled loose.

Everyone applauded or laughed or smiled. Everyone, except the bola man. The whip man nodded to everyone.

"Buenos noches!" the whip man yelled with a hand in the air and an almost smile. He rolled his whip into loops and hooking it onto the modified belt holster.

"So!" The bola man shouted.

Gunther and Jefe exchanged glances.

"SO! If we stood in front of each other. You with your whip. Me with my bola. On our belts. And we...struck...who would win?"

"Win?" the whip man asked.

"Win!" the bola man said.

"I don't know," the whip man said smiling.

"I think that bola would win," one man said.

"Okay," the whip man agreed calmly.

"You don't believe?"

"I don't know. I don't care," the whip man said.

"Why don't we find out," the bola man said stepping away from his group, as though he was going to duel in a showdown, gunfight.

"I think I would hurt you. Where am I supposed to hit you with my whip? You senor, you would only wrap me up. I...I have a whip."

The two man stared at each other. The onlookers were silent.

Then one man shouted, "I bet 5 pesos the whip man wins."

"What do you have to lose, Latigo?" the bola man said.

"I do not want to whip you, amigo. Whip your face. Whip your arms. Neck. Heck. This really hurts. It could leave a deep scar. A scar on you. It will hurt very much. Even if I lose, the whip can still hit you."

"Oooooh, so you do not want to hurt me, huh?"

"Si, senor," the whip man said with that same cordial smile.

They stood silent. Facing each other. This evolution, the escalation was now...inevitable.

"I sez dat the man with de bolo wins! 5 pesos," one man said.

And some other betting began.

The two stood there facing each other. For any onlooker, any person watching, it was hard to tell what sparked it. The spark was visible only between those two men. A flinch? A shoulder quake? Finger twitch? Both had their plans. The bola was to wrap the whip man's arms and torso. The whip man was to get his arm up high and away from this torso wrapping. Both men uncoiled their tools, but the bola had to be spun at least once?

Both went for their weapons. The bola man his. The whip man, this Texas Ranger spy, for his. The bola took to the air, but the whipping arm was up and on its way and the whip tore through the air above the chain saw of three incoming stones on cords. The bola did capture the whip man's left arm and torso, but the whip snapped open the head of the bola man. It cut the flat brim of his hat and sent it flying, and sliced across the top of his forehead. The whip man had little control over the impact because of the hurried delivery.

Everyone gasped and the bola man fell to the ground. His friends rushed over to him.

The whip man unwrapped the bola from his one arm and torso. He walked to Javier and handed it to him. The wounded man was too dazed to really know. Then the whip man started to coil up the whip as he stared at the downed opponent. He remained expressionless. The group hauled the bola man over to the sidewalk and propped him up on the steps. He was senseless, but alive.

"His eyes okay?" the whip man asked.

"Si," a man replied. Another man slapped at the bola man's face, trying to fully wake him up. The slice was bleeding from the top of his head.

"Okay. I hope he is okay," the whip man said.

The whip man crossed the street to Gunther, Jefe and Calabash. He put his boot up on the tall sidewalk, pulled a smoker's kit from a pocket, struck a match and lit a pipe. He was much bigger when close up. About 6'3" and stocky. He took a deep draw on the pipe.

"Evening gentlemen."

"Evening."

"Good evening. Yes sir. That was some exhibition," Calabash said.

"Amen to that. I apologize. That was unnecessary to see. It was a strange encounter with a strange ending. My name is Sam Bush, pilgrims," he said. "Y'all looking to join up with the Revolution?"

"No sir," Gunther said.

Sam Bush seemed relieved about that.

"You seem to be a smarter feller than to do such a thing," the whip man said.

"I am. We are," Gunther said. "We are here just to buy some guns for a security job east of here. Then vamoose. Hopefully tomorrow. How about you? You joining up?"

"Yes. I have a little experience in such matters, and I thought I'd be a 'soldado de fortuna,' as they say. That seems to be what they call them now."

"I am thinking we came here at the wrong time," Gunther said.

"Wrong time?"

"Yeah, with Villa being here and all."

"Ahhh, yes. I see. Could be. You stayin' here?" Sam Bush asked, pointing a finger in the air.

Though Gunther knew him to be Bullwhip Pierce. Gunther didn't react to the false identity. It just confirmed his suspicions.

"Yeah Sam, we are."

"Nice!"

"Yeah. Nice enough. Where you staying?" Gunther asked.

"Roast Pot Inn," the Ranger said.

"Nice?"

"Nice enough too." He puffed on his pipe. "Know where there's a good breakfast? I'd like to get away from the crowd a bit come morning."

Just then a loud, whining mechanical sound pierced the air coming from the south. Everyone cranked their heads in the direction of that alien noise.

"What the hell?" Calabash said.

"NOW, sir!" Sam Bush said to Calabash over the din, "I don't abide well with cursing in my presence. It sours the Lord's air."

The man objected to the word "Hell" in his presence, and Calabash caught on.

"Well, I am sorry, sir," Calabash had to almost shout as the terrible noise got louder. "I believe I'll listen to any man, that can split the eyebrow of a man with his whip."

A dark green truck with four oversized wheels, a rig almost as big as a conestoga wagon, turned the corner. Both Whittle teenagers and Rock Candy Randy burst out the hotel front doors astonished by the foreign sound, their heads swiveling east to west and back again, scanning for the source of the horrible screaming sound. The vehicle approached. A man dressed in white cranked a handle that spun something inside a cannister hanging off the passenger window that created the horrible noise. There were big red crosses on the front and sides.

"That pilgrims, is an am-bu-lance," Bullwhip/Sam Bush said.

Gunther and Jefe had seen plenty in Ft Worth, but apparently Calabash and the Whittle boys had never seen nor heard such a thing.

"An ambull-ance?" Whistler said. "What does it do?"

Two Hispanic men jumped out of the truck with little bags in their hands and ran up to the bola man, who was now half supine on the sidewalk.

"They're doctors, young fellers," Sam Bush said to the boys. That's what they call a siren you heard, and it clears people, horses, cars - what have you - out of the way so's they can get to the wounded fast. Hurts your ears, don't it?"

"No sense racing to the dead, I guess. They're dead," Calabash said.

"True, but the souls of the dead will be racing to Heaven, Hades or Purgatory," Sam Bush said. Then he turned to Gunther and continued, "Villa has stolen six ambulances from the Mexican Army. He takes one with him everywhere he goes, should he fall ill. Villa is very afraid of assassination. He changes where he sleeps every night, several times. The doctors are, well, essentially kidnapped, and while they no doubt prefer the Mexican government and stability, they act like they are only in the healing business and will heal any and all ill or fallen folks. Renegades, Revolutionaries. etc."

"Somebody must a run to get them. That's a big to-do for a little ol' whipper crack atop a noggin," Calabash said.

"I am sure it hurt him a plenty. I was trying to out draw him, and I lost some control cracking it for the speed. I'll bet that is quite a cleavage on his scalp," Sam Bush said. "But you know...the devil wears a goatee. That man from Brazil has the wrong facial hair."

"What...did we...miss?" Whistler said?

"A whip versus a rope-with-rocks showdown," Calabash said.

"The whip won. Slung by this here Christian."

"Elegants for breakfast," Jefe offered up to continue the prior conversation. "It's over... it's... well... ask your clerk and he'll tell you where it is."

"Excellent. Elegants. I have to get out of here before the Day of the Dead Parade marches through. Too much devil and death for me. Not a celebration of life. Though the good book says it might take some time before one rises or falls. Maybe I'll see you there in the morning?"

He looked right at Gunther with a raised eyebrow. He put his foot back on the street and started off. "I'll probably be there at about 7 a.m. May God bless you, gentlemen."

"Goodnight, Mr Sam," Calabash said.

"Buenos noches," Jefe said. Jefe looked at Gunther. Gunther barely nodded back.

"I'll be there," Gunther quietly reassured Jefe.

"There's a parade?" Whistler asked.

"Yes," Jefe said. "The Day of the Dead Parade. People pray for and remember friends and family members who have died, and this helps their spiritual journey. Día de los Muertos. I would have come for you boys. I would not let you miss it."

"I've heard of this," Josh said.

"I haven't," Whistler said.

"Cause Dad never took us. Dad said it was too scary."

Rock Candy Randy had fetched a metal coffee pot and poured Gunther another coffee.

Calabash lifted his near empty glass in the air, shaking it. Randy got the message.

"Randy?" Gunther asked, "Do you still have the same Marshal here?"

"Yeth, sir. Marshal Hethston."

"Okay."

"I ain't never seen a little showdown like that," Calabash said. He explained what happened to the teenagers. They sat down on the wooden patio, cross-legged and listened as they watched the bolo man being hauled off the steps and into the ambulance.

"Wonder where Marshal Heston is?" Gunther asked. "Wonder why he wasn't patrolling around this dinner, watching over this wild bunch?"

"Good thing he wasn't," Jefe said. "Try to imagine him stopping the castration of Zamora, surrounded by all of Villa's soldiers."

"Yeah. That would be some tough police work," Gunther said as he watched Sam Bush - or rather Ranger Bullwhip Pierce - walk calmly away up the avenue. He wondered what was really going on with him? Here? With all this? Maybe he could find out in the morning?

"He's real religious ain't he?" Calabash whispered, as he turned to watch him too.

Gunther nodded.

"You suppose he did all that, because the man had a goatee like the devil?" Calabash asked?

"No," Jefe said. "But...but I don't think the goatee helped."

Villa emerged, lemonade glass in hand, from the Rotunda with a rumble of noise and a small entourage. Guards, some local men, women and waiters poured out after him. The waiters hustled nervously trying to get all the people in chairs along the sidewalk in front of the restaurant. Then they took orders.

Villa spotted Gunther from across the street, smiled and waved. Gunther waved back.

"Your new friend," Jefe said.

"My new friend," Gunther said.

The parade was soon to begin. Men, women and children slowly walked into view, standing on the sidewalks. Some in costumes representing the dead. Some not.

"Boys," Jefe said, "you see that man across the street with the moustache and big hat?"

"Which one?" Josh asked.

"The man in the middle...drinking from a glass right now."

"Yes."

"Boys, that's Pancho Villa," Jefe said. He did not point Villa out at the gun store earlier in the day, but Jefe thought it was time to.

Josh leaned forward for a closer look, "Really?"

"I heard of em. Daddy's mentioned his name but who is he?" Whistler asked.

"He is a general in the Mexican Revolution," Jefe said. "He is famous, and someday you can brag that you saw him in person."

In the distance, came the music. Mariachi band. Drums. Some singers. The marchers were dressed in patterns of bright colors. There was a float of fake skulls on wheels, some of the shulls 10 feet tall. A man dressed in black, on stilts struggled up the streets. Dancers swirled. Dignitaries that Gunther did not recognize walked amongst the action.

One woman held a skull face mask on a stick before her face. She removed the mask when she saw Gunther sitting on the La Contessa patio and she smiled at him. He smiled back.

"Yet another new friend," Jefe said, somewhat in disgust.

"Just an acquaintance, amigo."

Villa grinned and drank his lemonade. Pointing, waving and laughing at the parade as it went by. It seemed he was the guest of honor. Gunther stared at him, not the parade, thinking about Celesta's warning. Villa was capable of anything, at any time. Would he, could he turn against these people treating him like a king? Gunther looked down at the wide-eyed, Whittle boys. Could he and Jefe, and now Calabash, keep them safe?

Hercules from the gun store came next in line, dressed in skeleton colored clothes, his face painted with black and white stripes. He pulled a wooden platform on wheels with a thick rope over his shoulder. A barbecue cooker, shaped like a big revolver was on the platform. Atop the cylinder of the gun-shape part sat Chueng, also dressed like a skeleton, waving at everyone. Atop his lap, a guitar. When he wasn't waving, he strummed the guitar. A sign for his store hung on the side of the deck.

"That's the big, strongman from the gun store," Josh said, wide-eyed.

As the parade moved on and on, some men on horseback were riding up the sides of it, like an escort, or security. They were in normal clothes, hats and wore badges. Gunther recognized Marshal Preston Heston. He sat tall in the saddle with a double gun belt, and none too quick to smile at the crowds.

"There's the Marshal, Nister Nunther," Rock Candy Randy said.

"Yup," Gunther said.

"This parade ain't so scary," Whistler said.

"Don't tell Daddy," Josh said.

Chapter 8: Rancid Dreams and the Shaman Hexing of Johann Gunther

August 1924, Omaha, Nebraska

"That first night we all went to bed and I couldn't sleep," Calabash told Pershing. "Who could? I thought about Gunther's offer for a job. Why not? More money and safer and better than knockin' around in a war. I had a few snorts of a little sippin' whiskey and finally slept like a newborn. I dreamed about whips knocking bullets out of the air. Ka-SNAP! KA-snap! HA. The next day, well...something had happened to ol' Gunther. Gunther told me he'd had a hell of a bad, black magic night! Like somebody put a spell or something on him. He thought...he thought somebody got into his room like a ghost and put the heeby-jeebies on him."

"So you decided that you'd leave with Gunther and Jefe the next morning?" Lt. Hawes asked.

"Yes sir. But there was a serious postponement on that the next morning. Gunther...uncovered a small war."

****

October 1915, Tremboro, Texas

"Boys, return to your room and get some sleep," Jefe said at about 9 p.m. "We do not know what will happen tomorrow, so you need some rest to get ready."

They were excited hearing about the bola versus whip fight, the parade and seeing Pancho Villa. But, without hesitation they filed into the lobby then off to their room. Sleep would come hard.

From the north, Gunther spotted George Hall meandering down the street like a casual, sight-seer, in the company of some older, Mexican Revolutionary with his head swiveling around like a bodyguard.

"Good evening gentleman," Hall said when he approached. He stopped by the hotel patio. "Jolly good night out here tonight."

"It certainly is, sir," Calabash said, intrigued by the accent.

"Have you gentlemen read today's local newspaper? Much said about the Generalissimo's visit."

"I haven't," Gunther said.

"I am through with it. It's yours," Hall said and handed the rolled up newspaper to Gunther.

"I will have to read all about it," Gunther said calmly.

"Colonel Charming," Hall said, introducing himself to Jefe and Calabash. "I am with the General. And this is my attache, and...and strident bodyguard, Sgt Juan Redardo Delagard. As apparently I am so important, I need constant protection. More like supervision."

Jefe, wise to the true identity, stood and shook the Brit's hand. "My friends call me Jefe," he said.

"I am happy to make your acquaintance."

Following suit, Calabash bolted up and said "Willin Calabash, at your service."

"Hope to see you men in the war," the colonel said, working the line as if they would all soon be comrades. He tipped his hat and walked off slowly, Sgt Delagard in tow.

Gunther shoved the rolled-up newspaper into the breast pocket of his jacket. With this delivery, his night was complete.

"Good night," he said, stood and left the porch.

With each step, a certain dread, a depression deepened in

Gunther. Once in the room, he shut the door behind him and stood still inside. The room was cool from the early fall night air and open windows. He stared at the bed for a moment. Some nights, in some hotels, some of these dreadful and dangerous nights, he'd slept on the floor, somewhere near the door. Off in the dark, shifting around in the dark, like Villa did to avoid assassination. He kept a brace of pistols on the floor near his hands. He would puff up the bed to make it look like he was asleep on it, to fool anyone charging in and trying to kill him. He thought of the night, years ago when he was a Texas deputy, when two men burst into his room. They shot up the bed. He shot them up from the side of the room. He killed them, then had to flee the city

He turned on the electric lights. He didn't want to sleep on the floor tonight. There wasn't really reason to do so, just a feeling. But, he was growing worried about tomorrow. He felt...odd...about Celesta's warnings. He locked the door. The room had an attached bathroom so he was in for the night, unlike some rooms with one common bathroom down the hall. The bathroom even had a shower over the tub.

He took out the rolled-up newspaper from his breast pocket. In one moment he located within the three handwritten sheets containing George Hall's notes. His report to...the Crown. He didn't read them. Tomorrow he would. He really didn't want to get involved in all this mess. He shoved the report back into the newspaper and shoved it all into a side of the steamer trunk.

He swept off his hat and jacket, tossed them upon an ornate chair and walked to the window. The pine floor creaked with each step. The corner windows overlooked the main street as well as the side street. The lace curtains rolled in a lazy wind pattern. He snatched the sides and pulled them apart. The main street below was paved, the side street flattened dirt, much like the evolution of any growing, modern town. Paper and wooden skeletons hung from windows and storefronts. Some scattered parade trash blew about like lost ghosts.

What of this town? Gunther thought. What if Villa raided the place? And why...how...did Celesta know to bring up Africa? How could she possibly know about Africa - and his "Star of Africa" - that beautiful, amazing woman, and how she might someday return to him? She was dead! Thousands of miles away. Was Celesta for real? A real seer? A real psychic? A real Santa Meurta witch of witches? He shook his gaze and thoughts free.

He walked to his dented, beaten footlocker again and reached in for his book, *When God Laughs and Other Stories* by Jack London. He tossed it onto the bed.

Then he took off his boots and lay on the bed, and grabbed the book. A good Edison, electric bulb light was near. Every story from Jack London was about death in some way. The tale of a struggling old boxer. A ship captain willing to abandon a man who tumbled overboard. Like the science fiction of Verne and Welles, a story about hundreds of years in the future, when workers were not allowed to read books. Gunther read them, but slapped closed the book at about midnight. A horse and carriage clicked by outside, breaking the silence. He turned out the light.

He kept his clothes on. He dozed, then slept. The nightmares began...

It was like his war in Cuba.

Like his war in the Philippines.

Like the carnage in Afghanistan.

Like the screaming of people and horses. The body parts spewing blood, flying through the air. Men, women and children. But this dream took place on American streets, half paved. Half dirt.

Flayed.

Tortured.

Shot.

Stabbed.

Speared.

Explosions.

Cannons.

Gunshots.

Machine guns.

His Star of Africa - dead.

He was suddenly sinking under the water of the nearby Rio Grande. Suffocating. He dreamed of a revolutionary soldier holding a man's forearm and placing a pistol to the upper arm of the man and shooting. He dreamed of a soldier shooting a man in the knees and elbows. He dreamed of a soldier skinning a man alive like a potato. He was held back by soldados and could not stop them from this carving.

NO!

He awoke. Gagging. Sweating. Itchy. He sat up. Stiff. Sick. Was this some kind of spell hexed on him, these sights, these ideas, vomiting all around him? He got up and poured a glass of water from the pitcher on the dresser and drank it down. His watch showed 3:12 a.m.

Celesta could be right. Pancho Villa was cut off from American help. He'll leave tomorrow with his new recruits and when he does? He'll leave tomorrow with everything Tremboro has to steal. Everything in Tremboro he needs to kill. Or just feels like killing. The Butcher kills. Venzula kills. He's done this before to Mexicans and Americans living in Mexico. He murdered 600 Chinese miners and was damn proud of it.

Then he noticed his boots were not where he'd left them. They were neatly set side-by-side against the opposite wall. Did he leave them...over there? His pants and shirt were on the table and not draped over the chairs. Did he take them off? His hat was brim down on the trunk. He stumbled to the door. He turned the knob left and right. It only gave a bit. It was still locked. What...?

He moved to the windows. The screens were still in place. The street dark, as the lights were turned off, as so many cities do after the witching hour...he thought..."witching hour." The ambient moonlight rested in patches on the street and hung on sections of buildings. Some of those skeleton decorations danced and glinted.

Was there...was there a person walking down the sidewalk? Odd. No three. Three...gray...people. Three women in long dresses, almost...almost floating. Were their feet moving under those dresses? Stopping. Then starting. Their arms folded across their chests as if disgusted or impatient. They stopped and looked right up at him! Their faces blurred and as gray as a fog.

After a few seconds they turned and drifted out of sight. He was driven to the next set of windows to view more of the main street. The women were gone. What the hell?

Then his stomach convulsed. He lunged for the bathroom and vomited into the sink. It was a thorough vomit, his belly quaked in aftershocks. He sat on the wooden bathroom floor, and cursed a long string, as long as the drool string hanging from his lips. Then he crawled back to main room, put two hands on the dresser and stood, to turn on the light switch. He limped over to the bed and sat. He snatched the pillow, laid down and held it on his lap. He hammer-fisted it lightly several times, mindlessly in frustration. Then he took a good, hard look at the white pillowcase. It seemed a little stained? He lifted the pillow to his nose.

Rotten...vegetables? That's what it smelled like. Bad. Sour. A rancid stew. It did not smell like that when he first shut his eyes. Did it? Gross! He looked again at the pillowcase. Half of it did seem somehow discolored. Just a bit? Was his face sprayed or misted with some concoction by someone? Some witch's concoction? He got to his feet and while feeling foolish, he sniffed the air in several parts of the room. Really, nothing.

He walked back to the door, unlocked it to see if there were any signs of wood or paint chipping around the lock or frame. There was a distinct rattle when he pulled on the door. There, hung on the outside door knob, was a strand of rosary beads, a necklace like the ones Zamora tossed at them in the restaurant. What? Gunther stared at this abstract message. His stomach growled. Maybe he should have slept on the floor after all. He instinctively reached for the beads, then stopped, remembering the 'don't touch' warning from the Rotunda. He looked at Jefe's door across the hall. No such talisman hung from the knob. He looked further down the hall and found nothing hung on the boys' room door or Calabash's.

His gun belt was on the seat of a chair. He stepped to it, pulled the Bowie knife from its belt sheath and returned to the totum on the knob. He hooked the rosary with his knife and stepped fully inside, closing and locking the door behind him. He held the beads up to the light, feeling foolish, but still not touching the trinket itself.

"I guess I've been...hexed," Gunther whispered, "by a goulash of dead produce and tricksters." He shook his head. "That put me into a nauseous nightmare of a sleep. A witches brew. A trick of some kind."

With a flick of his knife, he tossed the beads into a waste basket in the corner. He leaned over and pulled a satchel from the steamer. He took out a packet of B.C. Powder and walked into the bathroom. He poured a glass of water and tapped the powder into it. He spun the mixture with the handle end of his razor. He downed the glass. Then he stared at his blank face in the wall mirror. Jaw hung long. Puffy eyes, half-closed.

The report from George Hall! He opened the steamer and grabbed the newspaper. He flipped it open to see Hall's hand-written pages still inside, unstolen. Safe.

Weak, he sat on the floor and looked the report over. George Hall recorded for his superiors the travels of Pancho Villa. He stated that Villa was an odd, power-crazed, impul-sive madman, whose personality switched to violence over any small thing. He was guilty of torture and crimes of war. A German military adviser had Villa's ear, and the ears of the Revolution. The German suggested to Villa that if Mexico would make war with the US? If Mexico would keep the US busy while they waged war in Europe, then next, the Ger-mans promised to move on the US and give it all to Mexico.

Gunther laid back on the floor, half on the fringe throw rug and half on the wooden planks. My God, he thought, how many people were there in Tremboro? How many families?

Children? Miners? Water appeared in his eyes. Ranchers? Farmers? Stores? How many could be kidnapped and ransomed by Villa? Why did Villa ask Chueng about the "rich' people and their big houses? How many will be hung from the telegraph, telephone and electric light, street poles? Piled in heaps on the streets? He had seen all this before, around the world. He knew Villa ordered these same things before.

He gasped. And Fierro, the butcher was there. Venzula. He shot up to his feet. His headache pounded. Dizzy. He thought of Venzula's face inches from his by the horse, and the abject evil behind that face. That brain. That heart. Those eyes. A man that would cut a horse's neck for no reason but sheer torture?

He ran a hand through his hair. It felt sticky. He smelled his hand. It reeked of that foul smell. Would all this even happen? Tomorrow? Just what in the hell would happen tomorrow? How would Villa steal and kill a city? Should he, Jefe and Calabash just leave in the morning? Save the boys. Or, should he stay and fight? How would...he...really dizzy...again. He sat. He passed out on the floor from exhaustion.

He dreamed about shamans, witch doctors and warlocks. He was hung by his ribs like an Apache in a rite of passage. Indians chanted in a circle around him, but Celesta was there too. She shook rattles and shouted advice in Spanish to his bloody face. Words he could not translate.

"Mátalos! Mátalos" she yelled over and over again in Spanish.

"Mátalos!"

Chapter 9: An Inelegant Breakfast at Elegants

Tremboro Times Daily:
"It was a tremendous night of activity and gaiety at the Rotunda Restaurant with The Great, Great Generalissimo Pancho Villa and his distinguished officers in attendance. Most of the Tremboro Chamber of Commerce were there, as well as the mayor, the city council and managers of the Quicksilver Mine. Also participating in the dinner of honor was a number of North Americans, South American and European volunteer recruits the general needs to continue the great cause. Viva la Revolution, I say!" - Hardy Thompson, Society Editor

****

Gunther's group, men and boys, congregated in front of the hotel early the next morning.

"I am taking these boys to breakfast," Jefe told Gunther.

"I'll be..." Gunther said.

"I know," Jefe said. "Breakfast with the whip man."

Gunther started to walk off to Elegants Restaurant, then said, "Remember, don't go to Farleys. They wouldn't let you in last year."

"Scoundrels," Jefe muttered. "We won't."

"They wouldn't let you in somewheres?" Calabash said.

"No. They thought I was Mexican. Half this city must be upset with all these Mexican soldiers and Villa going any- where they want. Like movie stars. It breaks their rules."

"You ain't Mex. You're a Filapeenio person."

"Happens to me all de time," Jefe said. "At first, Gunth would get mad and there's been a fight or two. I explain. He explains. And then, most times they let me in. But now, we almost laugh like it's a joke. Almost."

Within minutes, Gunther entered Elegants and sure enough, "Sam Bush" otherwise known as Bullwhip Pierce al- ready sat at a table. He smiled and waved Gunther over.

"Have a seat, Johann," Bullwhip said, tapping the ashes off his store-bought cigarette.

"I will."

"Coffee?"

"Coffee."

"Coffee!" Bullwhip shouted toward a waitress.

"I can only guess why you are here," Gunther said.

"You can guess part of it."

"Ranger business."

"If you must know," Bullwhip said, "I am not a Texas Ranger anymore."

"No?"

"No. I work for the New Mexico Mounted Police. Essen- tially we are rangers. Work for the governor."

"What...what happened?"

"Politics. Texas politics. Bad pay. Changing governors. Terrible quartermaster. I get $720 a year right now with New Mexico. But I tell ya, the politics are bad there too, but not as bad as Texas. No escapen' the politics."

Gunther half smiled and nodded.

"I am here, as you might imagine, spying on Pancho Villa for our governor."

The coffee came, along with Bullwhip's breakfast. The waitress set the plates before him.

"You know what, ma'am, I'll have the same," Gunther told the lady.

Bullwhip lowered his head and mumbled a prayer. Then he took a long draw on his cigarette and pulled it in deep. Gunther watched, thinking he likely sucked that tobacco down into his boots before letting it steamroll out.

"The governor has heard from the President of the United States that the Germans are making moves into Mexico. Trying to get the US distracted away from what is a brewin' in Europe. The Germans want to entice Mexico into a war with us. You've been keeping' up with yer ol kinfolk over there in the Fatherland?"

"Yeah, I read about it," Gunther said. "People think the Civil War here was bad. They should read about the history of Germany. The history of Europe. There's been a civil war just about every three years for centuries."

Bullwhip started chowing down.

"Yer kinfolk are pretty militant."

Gunther didn't comment.

"What's that crooked Ranger Chester Winch up to in yer hometown?"

"He's always up to no good, no doubt," Gunther said. "If I don't have cause to butt heads with him, I lose track of him. He must get real busy stealin' money, or running a scam somewhere. Our paths will cross again. It's inevitable. He hasn't tried to kill me since he hired that mobster Gawdy Shirtz, to bushwhack me at the college sports lunch."

"And the inevitable will happen," Bullwhip said with a real sloppy mouth full of eggs, as he ate.

"I hear talk," Gunther said, "that Villa is about to rape this burg for all its worth."

Bullwhip stopped eating and looked up at him.

"Typical Villa, ya know. If he sets his mind to it," Gunther said.

"On a whim," Bullwhip said.

"Whim."

"What you gonna do?" Bullwhip asked.

"What you gonna do?" Gunther asked."You're the law."

A plate of food arrived for Gunther. Bullwhip watched for Gunther to say grace, but he didn't. Then he sighed and just continued eating.

"My job here is important. More important than...this little burg," Bullwhip said. "Important to America. Important to the world. If he decides to...to attack Tremboro? I don't think I can interfere."

Gunther stared at him.

"I myself won't do anything...anything to hurt anyone," he continued, "but I...but I can't interfere with...well, I need to stay on as a spy."

"And if I put a bullet in Villa's head?" Gunther interrupted.

"Then it's over. But that ain't easy, man. He's always surrounded by an army."

They ate. Drank coffee.

"You do that? Kill Villa?" Bullwhip added. "And I think you'll change world history."

They ate more. Drank more coffee.

"So, what *you* gonna do?" Bullwhip asked.

"I'm gonna finish these eggs, then I'm going over to the telegraph office. See if the phone lines have been cut. See if the wire lines are cut. See if the train tracks are blown apart somewhere. That is typical Villa strategy. Isolate. Then rampage."

"Uh-huh."

"If so? Then...then I'm gonna raise an army of people around here to defend themselves. I'll start with the Marshal. Preston Heston."

"He's been scant."

"Yeah. Saw him at the parade last night. But I'll start with him."

"Know em?"

"Met him before. He ain't a bad man," Gunther said.

"Just scant."

"Scant."

They ate.

"I think that Villa and his men are just out of the Marshal's means of handlin'" things," Bullwhip said.

"Yeah. You know that if they've blown the tracks and cut commo lines, and they start hanging men, women and children off the lamp posts on main street, raping, stealing, burning down Tremboro, and the Butcher starts lining people up to test how his bullets will go through them? Well, what you gonna do?"

Bullwhip stopped chewing.

"If that happens? I'll shoot Villa myself," Bullwhip said.

With that, Gunther sat back and took the napkin off his lap, folded it and laid it on the table. That was the answer he was waiting for. He stood. He threw some coins on the table.

"I got it," Bullwhip said.

"I got mine."

"Okay."

"Be around," Gunther said.

"I'm always around," Bullwhip said. "Have a blessed day."

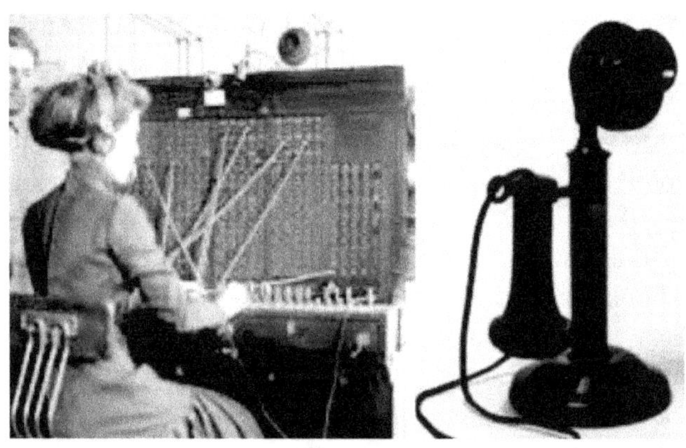

Chapter 10: A Sacking Like Rome
August 1924 Omaha, Nebraska

"It was that next morning the whole dang world went to hell, I tell ya. While we went to eat with the younguns'? Gunther predicted that Villa would attack Tremboro. Them Mexicans RE-volts were gonna kill us all," Calabash told General Pershing. "I even wound up a deputy of Tremboro, Texas. It was a black magic day in hell for everyone."

****

October 1915, Tremboro, Texas

"Good morning, sir," Gunther said as he opened the telegraph office door, ducking the overhead bell attached to the wall, above the frame.

"You're here early," the clerk behind the desk said. It was 8:05 a.m.

"Yes, I've been waiting for you."

"I *am* a little late this morning. Sorry."

"Since I'm the first one here, I guess no one has tried to telegraph anyone yet?" Gunther asked.

"No, not yet. I just unlocked the door and..."

"Try to telegraph...San Antonio," Gunther said. "Austin. Anyone. Anywhere."

"Any...where? Well, what's yer point?"

"Just try. I'll pay for it. Try. Tell someone you know, 'hello' in San Antoine. In a shop like this or where you know they will answer you back real quick. Austin. Wherever."

"I'll ask about the weather, then," the confused clerk said and shook his head. He tapped out a short message.

Jefe and Calabash walked into the shop and leaned on the counter next to Gunther.

"Be right with ya in a moment, fellers."

"They're with me," Gunther said.

After a bit, the clerk said, "Well, I'll be damned..."

"What?" Gunther asked.

"Well, well...there must be a problem. Must be a line down or something. I wrote to three offices up north....that..." he pulled out a pocket watch for a look. "...that should be open fer an hour by now. Dead. They are in our link-up."

"Try the phone. Get the operator," Gunther said.

The clerk reached for the phone, cranked the wooden phone box, put the ear piece to his ear and spoke into the receiver.

"Peggy? Peggy?"

Gunther and Jefe exchanged glances.

The clerk looked at them and said of the city phone switchboard operator, "She's there. Phone works."

"In the city, yeah," Gunther said, "tell her to call...tell her to call San Antonio."

"Peggy, we are checking the phone lines....yeah...yeah...our telegraph line is down. Peggy call the operators in San Antonio for us, will you?"

In a moment he turned to them and said, "Peggy said she can't reach San Antone. She says the line must be down too."

Gunther grunted and nodded.

"What?" Calabash asked.

"Tell her to connect to the railroad station office. Do they have workers at the station."

"They have four lineman. Twelve hours a day and on call. They..."

Gunther leaned in to read the clerk's name tag.

"Harry, I think Villa cut the lines and he usually cripples the railway to keep help from coming. I think Villa's gonna raid your town this morning. Tell the rail men to get here fast. This is an emergency."

"Who's to do such a thing? Villa?" Harry said.

"Villa! He and his small army," Gunther said.

Harry called, explaining the predicament on the phone.

"The boys?" Gunther asked Jefe.

"Back in their room. Frisky. Want to do something," Jefe said.

"Larry Barone and Archie Christian will be here in just a moment," Harry said. "I told them it was an emergency."

"Get the Marshal. Get the Marshal here if you can," Jefe said.

Gunther stepped outside and paced in front of the shop. The streets were quiet. A few cars. A few horses. A buggy or two. Folks walking to work. Two of the four ramline showed up within minutes, walking right past him and into the office.

In a few seconds, Marshal Heston and a deputy walked up. Brown uniforms, tan hats and black gun belts and boots. The deputy carried a lever action rifle. Silver star police badges on the shirts, not civvies like they wore the night before in the parade. They'd professionalized their look.

"Marshal," Gunther said, "I think we have a big problem here."

"Hello, Gunther," Heston said. "What's the problem?"

Gunther nodded his head to the door, for them to step inside.

"Look, my name is Gunther," he told everyone. "This is Jefe. We are private detectives from Ft Worth..."

"Pinkertons?" asked a railman with a name tag that read Archibald Christian.

"No. We're here on other business."

"And I'm with them. Name's Calabash."

"You ramline obviously know that Pancho Villa and his men are here in town. Right?"

"Yeah," said Archie.

"Yeah, of course," said the other, with name tag of Larry Barone.

"Look, they are notorious for raiding cities in Mexico. And the border towns, also a bit in Texas and New Mexico. And raiding American ranches and farms in Mexico. One thing they always do, is cut the telegraph lines. Cut the phone lines if there's phones, and they usually wreck the railroad lines if they don't need the railroad themselves to escape, but that is usually in Mexico. The fact that the phone and telegraph lines to San Antone are down this morning..."

Marshal Heston looked toward Harry the clerk.

The clerk nodded.

"This is not good news, and I'll bet the 2 p.m. train coming in? It won't make it. I think the track's been blown," Gunther said.

"She'll derail," Archie said.

"That's what they want. They don't want any...any reenforcements coming in. And a clean getaway for as long as possible."

"How do you know this?" Marshal Heston asked.

"It just makes sense. And, Celesta told me. She's been visiting the men Villa has camped outside town."

"Celesta? Well, she's about as nuts as..."

"She's been to their camp. And, it makes sense Marshal. Villa has done this before, and the lines are down now. Here!" Gunther said.

"The lines *are* down, Marshal," Harry repeated. "this ain't right at all. Two lines down?"

"The lines run on a single pole all the way to San Antonie," Heston said. "Maybe a pole's down and ripped the lines?"

"*This* morning?" Jefe said.

"Okay. Okay. Phone and wire down. Damn." Heston said. "We don't know about the track."

"We've got a 4-man handcar," Barone said. "Archie and I can pump down the line and see if they've damaged the rails."

"It won't be too far out. Just a good horse ride north," Gunther said. "And, I'll bet the lines were cut near where the rails are cut. We gotta stop that train run."

"It don't take much to damage those rails. And it'll flip that train like a flapjack," Archie said.

Gunther turned to Harry. "Can you...do you have a way to connect with the ends of a cut line so we can tap out a message on the other end of cut lines? Get on the San Antoine side of the cut line and get a message out? Morse Code? Somehow?"

"Yeah, we...we can do that. We got an emergency box. Morse Code. We can crank it up for power with a hand crank. We could connect it to that other side of the cut line," the clerk said, "and we could send a message."

"Who here knows how to do that?" Marshal Heston asked.

"I do," Harry said.

"But we need you here," Gunther said.

"I can do this," Jefe said. "I know how this works. Remember in the Philippines?" he said to Gunther. "All those cut lines? How many times did Malmo and I splice on a cut line and tap out messages?"

"Yeah. Yeah," Gunther said. He looked over the two rail men. He needed Jefe there with him, but the odds were hopeless in Tremboro if and when a full raid began. Jefe could take the teens away from town too, Gunther thought.

"Yeah, okay. Okay. Take the boys, too. Take Black Magic and get two more horses from Harley Benz. Try and keep these railroaders in sight."

"I'll get the box," Harry said as he left the front lobby and disappeared into the back room.

Gunther turned to Marshal Heston and the deputy. Preston put a boot up on a lobby chair, looking concerned, but not totally convinced.

"They kill people," Gunther said. "They rob em. They hang people. Skin em, whatever they feel like doing. Torture. Kidnap for ransom. And they got the Butcher with em."

"I know," Heston said. "Let's send yer friend out there. They can Morse code San Antoine and Morse us back too. *If*...if the lines were cut and not chewed apart by some damn vulture."

"Marshal, I..." Gunther started.

"I know. I know. But, I can't scare everybody to death here over an idea. If this adds up to real trouble, I will warn everyone now, and wait for word from yer man."

"How many deputies you got now?" Gunther asked.

"Six. A county sheriff staff of two."

"Deputize?"

"I can deputize a good group I know. Then I can turn all the others loose to defend themselves. Our main cattle ranch has a good group of cowboys working for em."

"They'll go for the livestock for sure," Gunther said.

Harry heard that as he re-appeared from a back room with a wooden box and a canvas duffle bag. "I'll call the ranch," he said.

"Get em on the line. I'll talk to em. I'll warn em to get ready for trouble," Heston said.

"This just sends out a message, Mister..." Harry said to Jefe.

"Jefe."

"Mister Jefe. We won't know if they get it or if...or what a reply might be."

Jefe and Gunther nodded.

"Then get on our end of the line and tell us what you've found," Harry said.

"They'll try the bank," Gunther said. "The gun store for sure. Warn everyone you can, Harry."

"What about the mines?" The deputy asked.

"You think they'd steal...mercury? It would kill him eventually. And how hard would it be to sell?" Gunther said, thinking aloud.

"Maybe rob the mine office?" The deputy said.

"Possible," the Marshal said.

"They got security?" Gunther asked.

"Yup," the deputy said. "Some old-timers though. They don't do much. Not like at a gold mine. But, they all got guns."

"Call em. Call em all and tell em," Gunther said. "Villa's got about 50 men with him now. We got hundreds of folks here, so if we can warn them in time..."

Harry motioned for Heston to come around the counter and talk on the phone. He did and told his deputy, "Get back to the office and start calling."

"Will do," the deputy said.

Jefe had the box out on the counter. He examined it, nodded at Gunther, and stuffed the apparatus into the duffle bag.

"Men," Gunther said turning to Archie and Larry, "Pump on out there and see what you got. Wait for Jefe at the train station. He'll be there with two teen-agers. Jefe is one fightin son-of-bitch. In case you run into trouble, there's no better man to have. But, if you got any guns? You'd better wear em."

"We do have guns. He Mexican?" Archie asked.

Jefe shook his head, ever so tired of that question.

"He's Filipino. He's a soldier and a warrior. A war vet," Gunther said.

"Okay. We've got our guns at the station office. Our train's at stake, Mr Gunther. We can't have her run off line."

Jefe slung the duffle over his shoulder. Gunther and Jefe looked at each other for a few seconds. They reached out for what looked like a handshake, but instead their hands passed and they grabbed each other at the forearms.

"My friend," Gunther said quietly.

"My friend," Jefe said quietly.

"Bring help," Gunther said.

"I will."

"They probably blew these rails in the middle of the night. Try to get the kids out of here. Find the breaks and go north. Or...or well, you make a decision what to do, but I'll be alright here."

"Where you want me?" Calabash asked.

"Get all your guns. Go with the deputy. Go where he tells ya," Gunther said.

"Jefe, get us news right away about those tracks," the marshal said, interrupting his phone call to the mine office.

Then Marshal Heston left too, clearing the office out, leaving Gunther and Harry. Gunther looked out at the calm, morning, city street. People still going about their business, walking, riding, talking, heading to work, to eat breakfast and to shop.

"I hope you're right about all this," Harry said, rounding the desk and counter and also looking out the windows, wide-eyed.

"Oh, I hope I'm wrong," Gunther whispered.

"Yeah, that's what I mean," Harry said and returned to the phone.

Gunther's concentration fell on a priest in a black suit walking down the street. It was Father Columbus, head down, walking somewhere briskly. Gunther looked at his hands. The priest's right hand was indeed....missing! As Celesta said.

"What happened to Father Columbus's right hand?" Gunther asked.

"Yeah. Yup. Damndest thing," Harry said. "He cut off his own right hand."

"CUT if off? Why? Himself?"

"He sawed off his own hand at the wrist."

"What? Why?"

The folks at the church said he...he woke up one day...and he...I don't know...and started hating his hand? It's crazy. Columbus said that his hand...wasn't *his* anymore. That it didn't belong to him anymore and wasn't part of him."

Gunther, a reader of, and a bit of a student of Sigmund Freud's works, walked up to Harry at the counter.

"Wasn't his?" Gunther repeated.

"Yup. Said it wasn't his. He went on and on about this for

days. They caught him one time slamming his hand against the wall. And slamming a door on it. Then one morning, he cut it off. Damn near killed himself. They found him in the rectory. Almost dead. Took him to the hospital and saved his life."

"How's he acting now?"

"Damndest thing. The church committee says he's normal again."

"Celesta told me she cursed his hand. I wonder if she made that story up *after* he cut his hand off?"

"Don't know," he said.

"Guess we'll never know," Gunther said, and returned to the windows. He watched Columbus walk on out of sight.

"I've seen this kind of calm before," Gunther mumbled. "Before the proverbial storm. If the wires are cut and the rails blown up, sure sign there will be a bloodbath here. Probably by noon. Surely by 3 or 4 o'clock. How many banks you got here?"

"One. Graham National."

"Call em."

"Yeah, yeah. Peggy's calling em."

"Like a military raid. A sackin'. A sackin as old as Rome," Gunther said.

"A sacking like Rome," the clerk lowered his head. "I've never seen a war."

"I have. Too many. Is Marshal Heston any good these days?" Gunther asked.

"Heston has his good days. He can...miss a few things...sometimes we think on purpose."

"Yeah. Like the big dinner last night with Villa."

"Trouble there?"

"They almost cut Zamora's dick off."

"Ohhhh, that's...that's trouble worth missing. Imagine though, having to arrest Generalissimo Pancho Villa."

"Impossible," Gunther said.

"Impossible. Worth missing."

They heard a woman scream. A banshee, howling scream

not unlike that alarm on the ambulance. Down the middle of the street, arms flailing, the bald witch woman Celesta jogged, her face contorted and her gait unnatural.

"RUN! Run! Run! RUN!" she cried over and over again.

"She must know something," Gunther said sarcastically.

"She's a seer. She sees. Santeria. Black magic," Harry said.

No one outside seemed to pay her any attention.

"She do this often?"

"Only once. She ran around yelling about an earthquake."

"Yeah?"

"Yeah," Harry said.

"Well?"

"Sure enough, there was an earthquake."

"Hmmm," Gunther said

"How many doctors in town?"

"Several. We got a hospital. I know...I know...call em."

Celesta looked right into the office windows as she went by.

"Mátalos! Mátalos," she yelled over and over again.

"What's that mean, anyway?" Gunther asked.

"It means in Spanish...like...kill them all."

Gunther lost his breath and his bearings for just a second. The dream. The...dream. How would he know what those words meant? How could he have dreamed that?

Chapter 11: Life Slit, Like the Wire
August 1924 Omaha, Nebraska

"I went back to the hotel and got all my guns and ammo," Calabash told Pershing. "All we could do was wait for word from Jefe. When it came? To this day, I...I hate to think about what happened out there on the flatlands to them." Calabash's eyes filled.

****

October 1915, Tremboro, Texas

Black Magic trotted spry, true and blue with Jefe atop him. Every few minutes Jefe stood in the stirrups to see more of the rugged, rocky, yet fairly flat horizon ahead. Thirty-five yards or so off to his right, linemen Larry Barone and Archibald Christian pumped their open, rail car up the tracks, their necks also craning to spy ahead every few minutes. The Whittle boys were a bit behind and to Jefe's left, on their rented stable horses. Jefe could see the kids were real ranch boys, and they could ride. He would smile at them once in awhile to reassure them, but he was not at all happy. So far, the railroad track was fine, and the telegraph lines were all fine, stretched pole to pole to pole.

If the lines were not cut and the railway intact, Jefe had to decide what to do? Should he just keep going north to that little town they saw just south of San Antonio that they passed on the train just yesterday? Get the kids out of any possible Villa trouble in Tremboro? Probably. If it all was cut and blown last night? He would run the kids north for sure, leave them with someone safe? Then return to Tremboro.

This routine went on for about an hour, then Jefe stopped. The rail men saw him and stopped too. Jefe spotted a rolling lump of riders way ahead, blurry in the distance inside a shifting heat wave from the tan ground and scrub brush, an odd, almost mystical wave for late October.

Jefe hand-waved the boys over to the lineman. He reached into his saddlebag and pulled out his Zeiss binoculars. He saw the soldiers. He thought they would have worked in the a.m. hours of darkness for such a mission. But no. No. They were that stupid, or that confident? Or given serendipitous orders at 6 a.m.? There was about 12 or 13 of them that he could count. His chest swelled up with deep anxiety. Ugly, ugly decisions must be made and fast. With no good ending. Why else would they be out there? He turned Black Magic toward the boys and the pump car.

"This is it. They have done their work," Jefe said when he got close to the tracks. "Start back. Start back. I did not expect to see them here this late. Because, good military work would have them do this in the middle of the night. But no. Go back. Go back. I must ride on and connect the lines and send for help."

"And stop the next train," Archie said.

"And stop the next train," Jefe said.

It was clear the ramline were already exhausted.

Jefe could just sense death in the air.

"I am going to have to circle around them to the east. I hope they don't see me. You go now. Go fast. Boys, ride ahead of them. Get on the other side of the tracks. Head back to hotel. Ride fast ahead of them," Jefe said.

"GO!" Larry told the boys.

The two took off with very scared faces.

"Them soldiers will catch up to us," Archie said. "We can't pump that fast."

"I want to stay with you," Jefe said. "But, the men are not angling this way. Maybe they will see you as harmless, or not see you at all. I can..."

"No. No you gotta get that message through," Larry insisted. "The whole city needs help...we'll distract em. We'll thin em out, if they see us. And we can't have the next train derail. We need help."

"We can stall them for the boys to get away," Archie said. "The boys will have a good head start."

The two looked down at the rifles on the deck. They both wore pistol belts with revolvers.

"I will send the message, and I will gallop with all my heart back to you," Jefe said.

The men nodded.

"Allah be with you," Jefe said solemnly.

"And sweet Jesus be with you," Archie said.

The duo began the rigorous, backbreaking work to pump in rotating synch to get back home.

Jefe heel-kicked Black Magic off to the east, to flank and pass around the enemy? Black Magic took off like a race horse possessed, and Jefe could hardly hold on. He rode off into that odd, October, waving heat.

"Nuthster Nunther! Nuthster Nunther!" Rock Candy Randy, out of breath, searched the streets, yelling for Gunther.

Gunther was several blocks away, talking to the two Mexican ambulance drivers he'd seen last night.

"I hear that you men are...are hostages. Kidnapped."

"Si, senor. We once worked for de' Tijuana hospital."

"Well, I look around and I see no soldados. You are standing here free. You are in The United States of America."

"Si senor."

"Then why are you still hostages?"

"Villa will *keeeeel* us if we try to escape. Secuestrado! The Butcher or Venzula will keell us."

"If you will help with the wounded. The American wounded, if and when a fight comes today, I will help get you out of here. You can work in Texas. Stick with me. Do not leave with Villa. You will..."

"Nuthster Nunther! Nuthster Nunther!" Rock Candy Randy rounded the street corner.

"The nelegraph office!" Randy shouted.

"Be around for help," Gunther told them, and raced past Randy back to the office. Randy stopped and just bent over, panting, and rested his hands on his knees, his mission accomplished.

"What?" Gunther asked, bursting into the office.

"Ohhh bad news, Mr Gunther," Harry the clerk said. "Jefe found the wire cutting. Sent a message to San Antonio. The rails have been dynamited."

"Damn."

"So, he said he sent a message to San Antonio," Harry said.

"Well, that's good. You tell the Marshal?"

"Yes. I called Peggy. Peggy told him."

"What else?"

"Then he also sent me this...they ran into the Mexicans coming back. The ramline and the boys were to return here. He thinks they are in trouble, and he was going back to help them as fast as he can."

Gunther grimaced, then said, "See if the Marshal can spare some men to ride north. I'll go on ahead. Can't wait. Tell everyone you can, it's on." And he left.

Gunther ran through the streets, taking stock - he had three pistols in two gun belt holsters and a shoulder holster. His belt bullet loops were full and a box of ammo rattled in his jacket pocket with each step. In his right armpit hung two magazines for his Luger. He had his big Bowie knife. But, what of the two boys? Of Jefe? The railroad workers? Had he sent them to their...death?

He dashed into the showroom of the Harley Benz Car dealership. Peter was at the desk.

"Peter!"

"Gunth?"

"Remember I asked about renting a car yesterday?"

"Huh?"

"Well, I need to rent a car." Gunther pulled $10 from his wallet.

"We...we don't rent...cars...," Peter said while standing up and staring at that $10 dollar bill.

"Jefe and those boys that rented horses this morning? And some of your local ramline? Are in danger up north. Villa's men. I need to get there and fast. I need a car. And get ready to be raided by Villa."

Peter looked up at Gunther from the $10.

"Villa! Yeah," he barely mumbled. "Yeah."

"Which one?" Gunther asked while looking at the autos.

"That one would be best," Peter said.

And then Gunther turned back to him and said, "Oh...I need a rifle."

It took three hand cranks to start the car. Gunther climbed aboard and hit the gas pedal hard on the 1915, EMF five-passenger Touring car and made for the railroad station. He knew there was a decent turnpike that ran due north beside the rail line. The handcar and tracks would not be far off the road. The canvas roof of the auto was rolled back and down. He spotted Celesta on a sidewalk, and she made the sign of the cross on her chest as he drove by her. He hit the horn several times to clear the path of horses, cars and carriages.

The rail station stood empty. Gunther cut the wheel left to turn on the road north. He could reach 40 miles per hour in this machine and he meant to push for every inch of it. No cars or riders were ahead as far as he could see.

And after about 30 minutes, there they were! About 9 or 10 of the Revolutionaries in their big hats and the semi-uniforms he'd seen them all wear in Tremboro. They were in no hurry, nor in any formation. Just a loose band of riders. Their morning job was done. They set the city up for attack. Gunther pulled a revolver from his belt, his 1910, Colt Police Positive Special and set it on the passenger seat. He rested Peter's loaded, lever action rifle, a Winchester 1892, closer to him on the seat, next to a box of rifle shells. He hopelessly searched the landscape to see if the Whittle boys were with them? Jefe? Anywhere? The rail workers? Near them? But no. Was there a riderless Black Magic horse recovered for their Colonel? No. But, he could see two riderless horses towed by the group.

"Damn," he said. His heart sunk. This was not good.

The speedometer topped out at 40. He keep to the middle of the rough road. Half the horsemen were just off the road and to the left of it, the other half on the road. The land was still rather flat. Gunther slowly veered the fast car to the middle of the road, closing in on the men with every minute. He got closer and closer. To the left. To the left, and...

Soon he was almost upon them, he aimed the big Touring sedan to the center of their pack. They all stopped and the big sombreros twisted back and forth as they looked around and commented to each other about the incoming car. Their horses became skiddish.

Gunther did not stop, did not slow down. Forty miles per hour dead on. He grabbed the Colt with his right hand. The group split a bit and cleared the path. Gunther could now see their faces. Some looked astonished. Some angry. He was upon them!

He started shooting, hitting several of them. Just as he passed, as the men and horses struggled away, he shot one more man to the right and one more to the left. Despite the speed, he was very close, almost hitting one horse with the car.

He heard the men shout behind him. He blasted past them for one full moment. He heard gunfire behind him. He heard some bullets crackle and whistle by overhead. He heard some thuds in the back of the car. He turned the car in a big circle, sitting as low as he could. He got back on the road and drove for a minute. Then he slowed and circled around. He faced them again from afar. He stopped. He braced his feet on the floorboard, grabbed the rifle, and over the windshield, he took aim. The remaining soldiers were charging him now and from the distance shooting their pistols. Their rounds were falling short. He emptied the long gun into the pack.

Confusion reigned among them as a few more men fell. Even some horses tumbled and rolled. One rider bolted east, but Gunther's last round cut him right off the horse. Another rider had not been shooting, but remained in a full run headed right at him. The soldado pulled his pistol and started shooting, but his aim suffered from the gallop. Gunther picked up the pistol, rested the barrel on the windscreen frame and fired the big handgun once. The round hit the man in the chest, his shooting stopped, but onward he rode. His face came into Gunther's focus. An expression of surprise. Gunther shot him again, right into the expression. The body fell. The riderless horse continued on right past Gunther.

Five men were left, circling their horses, uncertain what to do. They knew there was nowhere else to go. So they charged too.

Gunther turned the big car around again and raced away north, this time on the flat roadway. He sat low and the thick, black canvas roof gathered behind him concealed him from their view. His plan? Run them ragged. Turn and shoot. A night lamp on the driver's side exploded, but he was quickly, once again, out of their pistol range.

A lone horseman appeared off to the northeast, a smaller man on a big black horse. The horse was at a full gallop and the rider atop glided in total grace with its every movement. It was...Jefe on Black Magic. And, it was time. Gunther couldn't help but muster a sinister smile. He turned to the left, and off the road. Then he turned again facing south, facing the charging revolutionaries. And he stopped. Jefe and Black Magic headed south, way off to Gunther's left. Gunther waited. He waited. Jefe was in position, east of the men, to flank.

Then Gunther pushed down hard on the gas pedal, to the maximum. He sat tall again, pulled his second Colt in one hand, wrestled with the steering wheel while he yanked his Luger out with the other hand. His two guns up and out and above the wheel. He held the steering wheel with the lower fingers of each hand.

The band rode on right toward him. When in range, Gunther shoved the Winchester rifle butt on the gas peddle, then he half stood. He squeezed the steering wheel between his thighs, and began firing. He glanced to his left at Jefe. Jefe had two pistols also out and firing as he charged. Some 16 to 18 bullets pierced the men and their horses from their fronts and left sides in just a few seconds. Their clothing and bodies tore apart. They dropped, coiled and twisted onto the hard ground. Three horses remained afoot, slowed down, and once riderless, stopped. Other horses stood off in the distance.

Gunther drove up to them. He stopped the sedan. He dropped the Luger magazine from the gun onto the car seat, and shoved a new one in, as he scanned the scene. Jefe off to his right, reloaded his guns as Black Magic stood perfectly still. Guns loaded, he raised them up. Covered by Jefe, then Gunther loaded the rest of his guns.

"The boys? The ramline?" Gunther shouted.

Jefe waited for Gunther to look at him. He shook his head, no.

And Gunther felt crushed in his throat. He gasped.

Above the idling engine, they heard the wounded men moan and the shot horses snort, growl and whine. Flies from seemingly nowhere, suddenly started to gather. A lone buzzard magically appeared, circling above.

Gunther left the automobile and walked to the carnage of flesh. Jefe stood guard high atop Black Magic. Gunther stepped from downed horse to downed horse.

"I am so sorry, big fella'," he said to each dying horse and shot them in the head. The standing horses finched but did not run.

"So sorry." Again. And again.

"A...mi...go," gasped one bleeding man, "Amigo. What...what? Who are..you?"

Gunther looked at him.

"You...ahhh. Americano Federale? Can you, can you help me? I...I am..."

"No senor. I cannot help you. I do not have the time," Gunther said. "You have picked up with a sorry lot. The wrong side. I don't have the time to help you or any of your amigos here. I have to go back to Tremboro and stop your friends. But I will not let you, and your friends, die slowly out here. And suffer."

"Ahhh...amigo..."

"So! *Your* Revolution is over."

Gunther shot him in the head.

Then he shot everyone else not yet dead.

He gathered up the reins of the living, unwounded horses.

Jefe dismounted and approached him.

Gunther was too hurt inside to talk about the boys just yet.

Jefe found a rope on a Mexican saddle and ran it through all the halters of the surviving horses. Then he remounted Black Magic.

"There are more men and horses in the...in the distance," Gunther said.

Jefe nodded.

"Back that way."

"Okay," Jefe said.

"Where?" Gunther finally suggested about the boys.

Jefe motioned his head back toward the tracks. Gunther climbed into the auto. He slowly-trailed Jefe and the horses to the tracks and a bit north, dreading their inevitable arrival. Jefe dismounted. Gunther followed suit.

He saw the hand pump, rail car on the tracks. He saw the two ramline dead on the car. Archie's corpse half hung off of it. His head dangling. His jaw bone, shot off, and hung by the soft, stretched flesh on the side of his face.

Jefe stopped.

Gunther looked the pump car over. There were some spent rifle shells on the platform and on the ground. Rifles gone. Both their holsters empty. No doubt their guns were snatched by the soldiers.

Jefe walked south and east, leading the horses. Then he leapt up on Black Magic and they trotted off. Gunther got back in the car and followed him.

In a few minutes Jefe stopped and slid off the black horse again.

Gunther stopped. He stood up in the front seat. He saw the two boys. Their bodies lay on a small hill in the loose, disarrayed positions of death. He sat back down and looked away. Obligated. to look. Compelled to look. Disgusted. Horrified. He stepped down from the car and walked over to them.

Their hats, boots and gun belts were gone. He dropped to his knees by them.

He touched each one.

He cried out.

He cried.

The flies had beat them there.

Jefe stood silently behind him, his clothes shifted in a new slight breeze from Mexico-way. The breeze moved the long blond hair of the teens.

"The hell of it!" Gunther said. "We're in *Heeeellllll*!"

Jefe walked up beside him. Gunther stood.

Jefe put a hand on Gunther's shoulder.

"This is...what Hell is," Gunther whispered.

Jefe turned to stand guard, to make sure all the soldiers both close and far were dead.

"I...couldn't save..." Jefe said.

"I know."

"I couldn't do everything, I had to send the messages..."

"I know. I asked you to go," Gunther said.

"I volunteered," Jefe said. "We had no choice, Gunth."

"No...choice," Gunther repeated, but deep down, he and Jefe didn't believe it.

Chapter 12: Shoot 'em Up and Bang 'em Down
September 1924, Tremboro, Texas

"It was such a terrible day," Mrs Inez Wisenhut said.

"We are very sorry for your loss," General Pershing said. "And we thank you for your time here with us. I know it must be hard to think about all this again. To talk about."

"It was. It is," she said.

She proceeded to recall the events of her husband Peter's violent death years earlier at the hands of Pancho Villa.

"Did Mr Gunther ever tell you he was going to kill the people responsible for Peter's death?"

"Yes, he did. He said he was going to try."

"And did he say specially that he would kill Pancho Villa?"

"Yes, he did. Yes, he did and I wanted him to."

"I understand," Pershing said.

****

October 1915, Tremboro, Texas

The two dead boys' bodies laid across the back seat of the car. Gunther once again drove all out, but this time it was south, back to Tremboro. Jefe could not keep up with his band of horses. Jefe would lead the horses back at a slower pace.They'd hauled and lifted the two rail worker's corpses atop two of the horses. Gunther noted the wedding rings on the fingers of the men as they tied the men in place over the saddles. They gathered all the soldado's pistols, rifles and ammo and piled them all up on the passenger floorboards of the car.

Gunther glared ahead at the outskirts of the city, looking for turmoil, smoke, any problems and listening over the engine for gunshots. Sounds of crime, sounds of war. None. He drove around the north end of the city and entered on the dirt road streets in route to Peter's dealership, in hopes that the townfolk would not get a horrible vision of the dead boys laying in the back seat. As he got closer to the business however, he spotted some people milling around out front. Men and women, hand-wringing and flustered.

He pulled in, away from the business, sheltering those against the shocking sight of the dead youths. He jumped from the car and jogged to the storefront. The front window glass was broken.

"Wha..." he barely said as he passed the small crowd.

A Hispanic woman he'd never seen before was inside doing something Gunther couldn't ascertain. He stepped in.

She looked at him.

"Is Peter..." he said.

"He is dead."

"Dead?"

Gunther looked down behind the big counter, He saw the stable boy kneeling next to a bloodied Peter, prone. Lifeless.

Gunther knelt and checked him over. Beaten about the face and neck. Cut on the arms. Shot in the foot. Blood on his shirt. He moved the already torn shirt aside. Shot in the chest.

Gunther looked up at the woman. She was shaking. Cold. In shock. In anger.

"Villa," she said. "He and the Butcher. They came here with some men an hour ago. They said they had just played golf. Villa toyed with Peter over buying a car. They wanted a car. This car. That car. His men pushed Peter around...," she started to cry. "First, they shot him in the foot. Then, then they did this."

Gunther stood up. He looked at the bloody hole in Peter's foot. A large truck pulled up outside. Two Hispanic men wearing black suits and hats ran in. Gunther read the sign on the vehicle, "Cravios Casa Funeraria."

"They stole two cars and left," she said.

The two men bent down by Peter, sweeping off their hats.

"Lo siento," one of the men said to her.

Gunther walked into the attached residence area behind the storefront. He saw a blanket on a sofa. He snatched it up and ran back to the showroom. He wrapped the shaking senorita in the blanket.

He then stepped outside to the small gathering crowd.

"Villa is going to rip this city apart," Gunther shouted to them. "You can either go home and load up all your guns and kill every one of those sons a bitches that dare you. Or...or you can get out of here. Go north. They have no reason to go north. And, any help we get will be coming in from that way."

The citizens mumbled and shifted around with the news.

"What should we do?" one elderly man said.

"Well, I wish you'd stay and help us kill them. But that's a decision for you to make. You do whatever you've got the stomach for. You do that. But got-dammit don't stand around here like a bunch of lambs. You haven't the time. *Go* somewhere! Do something. Call up everyone. Tell everyone."

An elderly woman said, "Shoot em' up and bang em' down." She looked at the man next to her, obviously her husband. He grimaced, and they all turned and left.

Gunther walked back inside. The two men in black lifted and laid Peter on a sales table. He approached the woman. He put his hand on the stable boy's shoulder.

"Have the police been here?"

"Yes, but they cannot stay," the boy said.

"I have one of your cars outside. I'm gonna need that car to help people here. I'll get it back when I can."

"Will you get them?" she asked.

"I'm gona try."

"Will you keel Villa?"

"I'm gonna try."

 He looked out the window and said solemnly, "I'm gonna try to kill them all."

Then he walked over to the men wearing black.

"You men from the funeral home, right?"

"Si, senor."

 "I have two boys they killed up north in the back seat of that car outside. Will you get them? Will you...prepare them?"

 "Si senor."

"I have to get them back to Brownsville. If I don't make it? If my friend Jefe doesn't make it here? They are the Whittles family just outside of Brownsville. The Whittles. They are a big family, own a big ranch, and are well known in the community."

"Oh, oh my," one brother said.

"Si. The Whittles," the other said.

"Si, I'll get them in our wagon," one said.

"Senora," Gunther said, "my friend Jefe will be here with some horses for you. They are yours now. And he has two bodies of the railroaders too," he shouted out to the caretakers, but they didn't hear him.

"Two dead men from the train station?" Mrs Wisenhut said.

Gunther nodded. "My friend Jefe is bringing them in with the horses."

"Tell these funeral men, huh? And tell Jefe to try and find me. I will be patrolling the streets in the car. And I'll go to the gun store."

"The gun store," she nodded.

"I am very sorry about Peter," he said.

He turned to leave.

"You will geeet" them?" She asked again.

"I will try."

Gunther helped the funeral men remove the bodies of the

boys from the car. He started the car and drove for Chueng's Guitar and Gun Store, not knowing what in the world to expect but trouble.

It was now 9:50 a.m. The streets were still quiet. Too quiet. Peggy the phone operator must have called everyone with a phone by now and warned them. He parked the big sedan in the empty lot next to Chueng's. He reached down into the passenger floorboard collection of weapons and shoved the guns around in a search for some better ones. He found two of the more modern revolvers and pulled them up. He inspected them. Still loaded. He reached for his hat and coat in the back seat, got out of the car and slipped them on. He shoved the pistols, crossways into his gun belt. He now had two pistols in a two-gun belt. Two guns tucked in the belt and a Luger in a shoulder holster. A knife, and he still felt naked.

Men laughed. Noises way up the street as horse hoofs slowly stepped on the paved road from the dirt road. Gunther counted some 10 soldados, approaching at a casual gait.

He walked into the store. Chueng was working behind the counter. Hercules loomed at his post up on the high platform in the corner. Two other employees were working in the guitar section. Three customers. One played classical music on a guitar.

"Where's your doorman?" Gunther asked. "Your door guard?"

"He doesn't start until 11," Chueng said.

"You hear?" Gunther shouted.

"Maybe trouble? Yes. The switchboard operator called us," Chueng said.

"Yeah! Trouble. And there's no maybe about it," Gunther said. "And more coming down the street right now."

"Well how do we know there will be trouble? They might just...just come in and buy guns?" Chueng said.

"Chueng, they cut the lines up north. They wrecked the railroad tracks, killed two rail men and they killed those two boys that were with me yesterday. They just killed Peter at the stables. What do you think, Chueng?"

"They...they..?" Chueng stuttered.

Hercules suddenly turned his table over in front of him with a loud thud.

"And there's 12 of them coming down the street right now," Gunther warned.

"Arm up and get back here," Chueng shouted to his employes.

Gunther looked up and asked Hercules, "That table solid?"

"Oh yeah," he said. "I made it."

"What you got up there?"

"Three shotguns. Four pistols. Two rifles," Hercules advised.

The two customers stopped roaming and stood still. The third still played the guitar on a stool.

The workers put on gun belts and stood next to Chueng.

"No. No," Gunther said. "Spread out. Get a shotgun each too. Watch out for crossfire and remember, that glass ain't stopping shit," Gunther said, shaking his head in frustration, pointing to the glass counters. Get low. Get away from the glass and kill em all."

Gunther looked at the three customers. One was an elderly gent, a well-dressed cowboy under a big black hat. One, a middle aged man in farm clothes. The third man, in his 30s, still massaged the guitar in his hands, rolled his head with the music, framed by long, raggedy hair and beard, and had about 7 days of bad road layered on his brown clothes.

"I suggest you men either get out, or get on board with this," Gunther said to them. "There's fixen' to be a shit-storm in here."

The farmer looked scared.

"The backdoor is thataway," an employee said when seeing his face.

The farmer backed out at a brisk pace. The older gent remained in place. He smiled under his long, gray, handlebar moustache and black hat and flipped his jacket back over his holstered gun. He leaned on a counter.

"Get that man some more guns," Gunther ordered.

The man with the guitar picked up the pace with his music. As classical as a guitar can get.

"Mister Mozart?" Gunther shouted to him.

He stopped playing and grinned like a wild man. He had a gold tooth up front.

"I'll kill any man for this here guitar," he said whimsically.

"You can have that guitar!" Chueng said.

"What's your name," Gunther asked him.

"Elvaughn Mellencholly," he said, ending it with a dramatic chord.

"And what's your name, sir?" Gunther turned and asked the gent.

"Samuel Selleck. At your sudden service. From business in Eagle Pass. Just passing through to Reynosa."

"Well, sir. It is my wish that you will pass right on through to Reynosa when this day is done," Gunter said, "and fix up Mister Mellencholly too."

An employee pulled another shotgun off the wall.

"I need fixen," and he sang. And he continued playing. "I need me some fixens'..."

"You men ever been in such a fix before?" Gunther asked.

"HA!" Mellencholly declared.

The gent named Selleck smiled again, throwing those waxed, moustache ends way out.

An employee laid a loaded shotgun and a pistol on the counter next to the two customers.

They all saw the soldiers now through the store front glass. Venzula led them. The men stopped, slipped off their horses, still chatting like they were going to lunch.

"Let's try not to shoot each other, okay?" Gunther said as he backed away to a distant counter. The defenders were smartly spread apart. An employee handed him a shotgun too, and he laid it on the counter.

"Ya just wanna shoot em as they come in?" Mellencholly said, still playing, still looking down at the instrument.

"No," Chueng said. "Maybe they just want to buy some guns before they leave!"

Gunther shook his head in disbelief.

"No," Gunther said. "We'd get only the first few through the door and about eight of em would scatter outside through streets. And, surround us and who knows what else. They're not leaving without guns."

"Not much of a plan," Mellencholly said.

"Kill em all when I say 'now,'" Gunther said.

"*That* sounds like a plan," Mellencholly said.

"Mother, Mother, Mother of God," Chueng said.

Venzula opened the front door.

Chapter 13: The Big Mistake of Octavio Histofa
December 1924, Austin, Texas

"Please state your name for the record, sir." Lt. Hawes asked.

"My name is Annhowser Pierce," Bullwhip Pierce said for the record into the Edison mouthpiece.

"And they call you 'Bullwhip.' Others in our inquiries about the Tremboro incident refer to a 'Bullwhip.' That is you?"

"Yes. That is my nickname. As I once carried a whip rolled up on my belt."

"You no longer do?" General Pershing asked.

"No, sir. My shoulders. I can no longer raise either arm up but half way. I can only blame the sin of obsessiveness. Using the whip. Using the whip. Practicing the whip too much. Both arms. Like a false god. Some people like to fish. Some target shoot. I worked the whip."

"And your past employment, sir?" Lt. Hawes asked.

"I was a Texas Ranger for 11 years. Then with the New Mexico Mounted Police for 9 years. Then back to the Texas Rangers where I retired. Another 13 years. The politics will break a man down. Test your patience and your constitution."

"Do anything now?" Pershing asked.

"I study the Bible, General. I help out at my church."

"It would seem you might be a full preacher," Pershing said, "instead of just help."

"No," Bullwhip smiled. "No. I cannot hoist that mantle. That responsibility. You see, God is everything. The word of God is the ultimate word. If I were a clergy, I would be impossible amongst the people. You are either fully in or fully out. I almost can't stand myself. My faults. I would make others stand full in the bright light. Even...even with my whip. When I had use of it. I once whipped a man for cursing. Thou shall not be, like me, in that position."

The room fell silent for a bit, digesting that testimony.

"And your involvement in Tremboro, Texas, Mr Pierce. Why did you...how did you..." Lt. Hawes asked.

"End up there? Sent there. Volunteered actually. The governor feared Pancho Villa roaming on our south border. Like a jackal leading an army of jackals. He knew several Washington DC officials and they decided they needed to dispatch a spy. A spy that could infiltrate the rebels and send pertinent information back on the whereabouts and the plans of Villa...and any plans of attacking New Mexico or anywhere in the US. Which as you well know, General, he did just that years later."

"Why you, sir?"

"I am familiar with Texas and Mexico. I am a...a serious man of...foundation. The man for the job."

"How did you meet Johann Gunther?" Hawes asked.

"I first met him in Ft Worth, Texas a few years before Tremboro. We were investigating a corrupt Texas Ranger. Gunther was a fine gentleman. An ex-lawman, but still a lawman at heart. Then, years later, I saw him on the train to Tremboro with a bunch of mercenaries looking to sign up with Villa. I gave him a wink not to identify me. He was clever enough to stay quiet. Then I saw him on the street later that night. Then we had breakfast and my truth be told."

"Did he say anything about killing Pancho Villa?" Pershing asked.

"As a matter of fact, he did. He came to me at that breakfast, very worried that Villa was about to raid the whole town
of Tremboro. Kill men, women and children. Rape. Steal
everything. Something you too would be worried about at the
time. And you have been later on."

"What did he say about killing Villa," Pershing asked
again.

"He asked for my help...in fighting Villa. I told him I
couldn't help him. My job was too big. Too important.
National matters were at stake. Then he told me if he killed
Villa, my job would be over. I told him, that it would. As I
supped on eggs, I listened to him, and I realized as a good
Christian, I could not stand by and watch the death of inno-
cents. As a sworn officer of the law I just couldn't stand
down. He got the mere suggestion from my face, as I verbally
committed to nothing."

"And the town was attacked," Lt. Hawes said.

"Indeed, yes it was. I've never seen anything like it. To
this day, it stands as my definition of war. A very hell on
Earth."

"Hmmm," Pershing said. "It's not in the history books as
an attack. You men must have done a good job shutting it all
down."

"That's thanks to Mr. Gunther. Not me."

"So, you think highly of Gunther?"

"Johann Gunther is neither saint ner' sinner," Pierce continued. "And if he or I might smite Pancho 'Vile,' - that's
what I called him, 'Pancho Vile' - instead of Villa...if he or I
did, I say, so be it. The Lord's word is against *murder*, like
criminal murder, as in a crime." Pierce leaned forward in his
chair. "As I have walked the face of this Earth, sir, seen what
I have seen from the Apaches, the Comach, the gangs, the
scoundrels, I can tell you sir, without question. Without question! Forgive me almighty Father for my sin of words...but
there are just some sons of bitches that need killing. And
'Pancho Vile' is one of them. And killing him is NOT murder
by the ways of the Bible. It's the Lord's work. Killing, not

murder, is sanctioned by our Lord in war, sir, in...in self defense. As I am sure you know. It is not a crime. It is not murder. It's righteous justice."

Bullwhip looked at all the faces of the men in the room.

"That morning, it looked like to me that Pancho Villa was staying another day. I reported to the spot just outside the city, where the other new recruits and his troops were gathered. All toll, there was about 50 of us. All on horseback, up and ready to go do...something. Maybe train cavalry maneuvers to test us out? But Villa was very busy, telling his colonels and captains what to do. The officers then told groups of men what to do. It looked like war planning to me. Last minute. Kinda' frantic. Then I knew what Gunther suspicioned was correct. They were gonna set this little burg on fire."

General Pershing nodded.

"There was no interview process! No oath. We were all in the Villa Army. Scoundrel and hero alike. We were still in the United States. I consulted with God then and there, General. What was I to do? What if I was ordered by these pirates to hurt or kill my fellow Americans in an act of crime. Villa had reconned the whole city for a few days, as a Guest of Honor, and thereby knew every place, every corner he needed to rob and who to kill. Villa told a colonel to take some 20 men and take the cattle from the Carter Ranch. Colonel Orotagon walked his horse over to a group of us and told us in Spanish. The Americans didn't savvy the Spanish. I did."

"So, Johann Gunther was right," the general said.

"He was, sir."

"Well, what happened next?"

"The colonel culled us out. About 10 Americans and about 20 Mexicans. We left the main group. Villa shouted some other orders behind me I couldn't hear. I turned around and I saw Villa, Fierro and that British officer Charming, and a few men left for downtown. I turned around again and saw Venzula talking to another group and then, they left for downtown too."

******

October 1915, Tremboro, Texas

There was no longer a need for the Carter Cattle Company front gates. The ornate, metal gates had been removed when they'd gone to rust. This part of the Wild West seemed tame enough, and the business was so brisk, women and men came and went, working day and night. The stone and cement walled enclosure remained, encircling the Carter Hacienda, as in the residence and company headquarters and barns, pens, some other housing like bunkhouses, workshop and auction arena. It was like an enclosed fort, except for the missing gates.

But, right after the early morning phone call from Marshal Heston, Carter wished he'd had those old gates back again and a whole lot more, like cannons.

"Expect a visit from Pancho Villa's men," the marshal said on the phone. "Expect to be robbed. There's a German and a Filipino here, detectives from Ft Worth, who say they saw the rail lines torn asunder and phone lines cut to San Antonio. Such is the hallmark of a Villa raid."

"Tell Ethel to be safe!" Peggy the Tremboro telephone dispatcher interrupted the conversation. She was such an eavesdropping staple in the community, no one seemed to care anymore if she listened in.

"This is just how Villa works. Prepare for the worst," the marshal continued.

Carter rang the front porch bells and got all his men together. He told them to load up their guns, get his and their horses ready. They'd always had the occasional cattle thieves, even horse thieves, but this time, it was...an army coming. Some of the men planned to help cover the cattle and the cowboys were already out in the nearby pasture. The rest stayed at the hacienda.

About two hours later, some vaqueros on the north wall walkway yelled out, "Mr Carter! About 30 men are coming."

"What they look like?" someone yelled back.

"Like a...like a Mexican army. All big, big hats and bandoliers."

"Are they running in?" Carter asked, anticipating a war raid.

"No, sir. They are walking in sir," the vaquero said.

"Hell," Carter muttered to his wife Ethel, in the double doorway of their home. "If they'd come a runnin' and whoopin', we could shoot them from afar."

"What if they just want to buy cattle?" Ethel said, wide-eyed and inches from his face.

Carter just shook his head. "I don't know, Honey."

Carter's cowboys lined up inside a corral fence on the west side of the dirt road that led up to the house and office.

The little army slowly walked their horses in the main entrance. The colonel and his rag tag unit scanned the cattlemen, all looking nervous, all at their ready, hats on, guns on and horses saddled, lining the fence. This was not at all what they expected. They walked up to within 10 feet of the Carter house, front porch.

"Senor Carter?" Colonel Orotagon asked with a giant smile. He had seen his mentor Villa work his smile and charm so well to offset strangers.

Carter stepped out into the sunlight on the front porch.

"Yeah," Carter said.

"Buenas dias, Senor Carter! My name is Colonel Orotagon. I am a colonel in the Mexican Revolution, under Generalissimo Pancho Villa."

A very skinny man prodded his horse up beside Colonel Orotagon. He translated the message from Spanish to English for him. The man did this with a strained skinny neck and a worried look of fear on his face.

Carter stood still on his porch, six steps high above the horseback visitors, his white shirt rolled with the morning wind. In his right hand, a large revolver. Ethel, a hefty woman, stepped out the front double doors of the hacienda. She was broad, wearing a bright print dress, the shoulders of which was covered with thick, long gray hair. She too held a pistol, but in her left hand. She stepped over to one of the porch columns and rested her forehead right on the inside of a white column.

"For the sake of the Revolution, General Villa...well, he, we need some cattle."

Spanish to English translation.

"Well then, come on down off your horse, come on inside, and we'll talk about it," Carter said.

English to Spanish.

"Ooooh, hooo, we...we do not have the time for a lunch, Senor. Muchas gracias. Mucho. But we are in a big hurry. We have such a big war to fight," Orotagon said. "We are leaving right now."

Spanish to English.

Carter stood silent.

"You see, we need...we need to requisition a portion of your cattle. I am sure you understand...our cause." He pointed to the pens inside the wall off to his left, where about 50 cows were in view.

Spanish to English.

"Just them," the colonel said. "That will do."

Spanish to English.

"Requisition. Requisition? Is that what you call it?" Carter said.

English to Spanish.

"Si senor. We have a very large army, thousands of men over the Rio Grande in Mexico. We need to feed them all the time."

No need to translate.

The ranch cowboys shifted. Each sentence grew worse for trouble.

"Why do you hold the pistola, senor? Is this your wife? Why does your wife stand behind the...the column. She is quite big you know, and we can see a lot of her on either side? We...we see her there. And with such a big gun!"

Spanish to English translation.

"The Southwest American, Northwest Mexico Cattle-men's Association said that last year, Pancho Villa hung Wingo Daily upside down on a rope and cut his throat! And then stole *all* his cattle! Near El Paso. Pancho Villa himself killed Wingo's son with a machete, and they stole off with his niece. No one has seen her since," Carter said.

English to Spanish.

No answer from the colonel. He just stared. He was out of fake charm.

"Is that what you call...requisition?" Carter continued.

English to Spanish.

"I know nothing of this senor," the colonel said.

Spanish to English.

"And therefore, we don't like any of you sons a bitches comin' around here, asking fer free cattle."

English to Spanish.

"Ohhhh, on no. You see...you see...we need the cattle to feed our men. You have here, some men, but many of your men, hmmm, I can see are Mexicans. Out on the range, with your cattle, we also see many Mexicans watching your cattle. Do you...do you think that these Mexican men will not side with the Revolution of their homeland? With the great Pancho Villa? If Pancho Villa fixes Mexico they can return to their families."

Spanish to English.

"Do you men want to meet Pancho Villa?" Orotagon turned and said to Carter's Mexicans in Spanish. "He is like...like Jesus to the people of Mexico."

Bullwhip Pierce worked his horse backward. He cut back through the men and when broken out of the pack, turned his horse to the right. He sided up next to some ranch cowboys lined up by a corral fence. This drew some attention from both sides. Bullwhip dismounted with a rifle. He tied his horse off on a post. He stepped away from the steed, and he put his boot up on a rail and rested his rifle on his lifted thigh.

The Carter employees as well as the new soldiers of the Revolution, looked Bullwhip over.

"I didn't..." Bullwhip shouted in a deep roar as he cut a piece of tobacco from a pack and fed his lower lip. Then he finished, "I didn't join the Revolution to kill Americans and steal American cattle."

The colonel did not turn around, but the translater did. He whispered a translation in Spanish.

"Tell the confused American that the Revolution needs to eat," the colonel told the translator, without turning around.

The translator began and...

"I don't need any translation," Bullwhip said. "I speak perfect Spanish. Classical Spanish in fact."

Horses shifted their feet. Even they could feel some bad magic in the air.

"I did not join this Revolution, and for the very first thing, the very first act, to kill Americans, kill their Mexican friends and employees. And steal American cattle." Bullwhip added even louder. He spit. "And I am pretty well sure that any American here thinks this is a mistake."

Three new American soldiers of fortune left the casual formation and rode over to join Bullwhip. They dismounted, also with their rifles in hand.

"Now if you want to BUY cattle from Mr. Carter, that is different," Bullwhip said.

The colonel rolled his lips around his teeth still not looking back.

"Senor Carter, we do not have the funds to make any purchase of cattle. We need the cattle for the cause. The Revolution."

Spanish to English.

"Or what?" Carter said.

English to Spanish.

"Or, we take what we need and shoot anyone who..."

Bullwhip Pierce blew the back of the colonel's head right off with a rifle round. The hat and head piece flew and spun, all hairy, hat spinning, spraying red.

Everyone was shocked into stillness.

"Best time to shoot a man is in the middle of his sentence," Bullwhip said calmly breaking the silence and working the lever action. Everyone glared at the dead colonel and then at Bullwhip, all in a state of shock.

And then the bullets flew from the fence line from Carter's men into the Revolutionaries. Carter ducked low and fired six rounds into them also. And Ethel raised her pistol, peeked around the column and cracked six rounds their way.

Some soldados and a few of the American and foreign mercenaries still in the pack were able to turn their horses around and head for the entrance. Bullwhip's rifle ran out of ammo. He dropped it, pulled a pistol and shot one of them right off his horse.

"Get em' all," Bullwhip declared aloud.

An agile Carter vaquero leapt atop a fence post, hauled himself onto the border wall walkway, drew a rifle bead and killed another. Most of the men still got away at full gallop.

"THE CATTLE!" Carter cried out. He guessed that other revolutionaries were standing by at the grazing fields.

Some of the cowboys got to their horses. Carter ran for his and yelled, "You all are hired!" He yelled to Bullwhip and the others.

Carter climbed on his horse. His wife ran behind him, reloading her pistol.

"Any of these Americans that live?" He swung the gun barrel over the downed men and horses." If they live? Hire em' too."

"What of the soldiers, Mr. Carter?" a man shouted.

"Do as you wish," Carter said as he and a band of cowboys charged out the gateway.

Bullwhip stepped up.

"Do as you wish and I wish," Bullwhip said, "that we fix up who we can and send them back home. All of these men are not bad. Just some of their leaders. Show them the best of God's mercy."

The remaining workers looked at him, stunned, as he reloaded his rifle, while walking forward to look at the wounded and dead.

A wounded soldier, tried to reach for his dropped pistol.

"NO!" A nearby vaquero shouted. "No, amigo."

The soldier stopped.

"You do not need to shoot me, son," Bullwhip said to the soldier. "In Jesus name, I forgive you."

The vaquero translated. The soldier rolled over on his back with a painful sigh and released the grip on the pistol.

Household men and women came out to treat the wounded men.

"These...horses," Bullwhip muttered. And he circled the wounded ones, and shot each one that was gravely hurt.

Bullwhip looked out the gateway.

"I believe...I believe I will follow the good Mr Carter out to see about his cattle. See if I can be of some help."

Everyone still stared at Bullwhip. He noticed.

"My name is Bullwhip Pierce," he felt compelled to state. "New Mexico Mounted Police. Here on an assignment to spy on Pancho Villa, which is a ruse I am now done with. I now, resume my yoke as just a peace officer. And we don't take much to cattle thieves. So, I will be on my way to hep yer boss."

He got on his horse. The three former mercenaries also mounted, and the four men left the compound in a hurry.

Out in a pasture on a road to the Carter headquarters, Carter cowboys all stood at the ready, gawking over the landscape and their cattle, with their rifles in their hands. Six border collies stood on alert around them, as anxious as the men. The hundreds of cattle roamed idly behind them gazing.

"You hear that?" one said.

"I do," said another.

"Them's gunshots."

"They are."

"From the ranch house. Fer sure."

"Shit-fire and save matches."

All 14 hands got on their horses for a higher view, their heads craning in every which direction. There were trees, hills and open land and they failed to see any of the Mexican Revolutionaries anywhere yet.

"Maybe that Fort Worth, German feller was wrong," one said. "Maybe they ain't coming?"

"Then what's with all the dang gunfire? That's a helluva' lot of gunfire from the office."

Four or five of the men who'd been in scrapes before separated out from the others so as to avoid being bunched up.

Then came the sound of galloping horses on hardened dirt. Some riders were dressed like Mexicans. Some seemed American, hatless, galloping at full speed, appeared off in the distance on the west road. They disappeared into a dense grove of trees, but they did not reappear out the other end.

The men watched, confused.

"They're all still in there," one whispered. "Are they gonna gang up on us?"

"Those trees..." babbled another.

"This is it then," said yet another.

"This is..."

More galloping horses. Five more men appeared on the road riding hell for leather. The riders pulled their pistols and started shooting south into the tree line.

"That's Raoul with em," one said, recognizing one of their range bosses.

"And Mr. Carter!" one declared.

"Them bastards are still in the trees!" a cowboy said.

"That they are! To ambush Mr Carter! He's after em."

The cowboys lifted their rifles and started blasting away indiscriminately into the trees. The lever actions cranked away.

Suddenly about eight men on horses appeared out the south end of the trees in disarrayed flight. They didn't shoot back. And those men from the ranch house were still after them, but still a ways off.

A few more riders appeared from the ranch catching up with Carter's posse.

"Somebody's got to watch the cattle. This ain't over," the range boss said, scanning the pasture.

A moment for Octavio...

Octavio Histafa was born on the east coast of Mexico, 34 years ago. Close to the white sandy beaches of the Gulf of Mexico. His mother made furniture and his father made movie screens for movie theaters, for a successful local company. Octavio and his brother Ignacio were good students in school and their parents had high hopes for their futures. At the age of 8, Octavio started piano lessons with an all-consuming interest, which delighted his father, but his mother warned the father that Octavio might change his interest one day and not become a pianist.

"Estar preparado," she warned him. "The boy is young and he will change his mind."

Sure enough, when turning 14, Octavio wandered into a glass shop in his home town. He saw the many shapes and colors of glass vases, window panes and lamps on the shelves. Even glass sculptures, large and small. A woman inside the shop window spotted him. She saw his widened eyes and she stepped to the door,

"Would you like to peek inside?" she said, and pointing to the back of the shop. It was a magical place of rumbling noise and great, blasting heat.

He walked in with her and Octavio would always say that his life changed that moment. He watched the three men and one woman make this amazing glass. They blew into pipes and made round glass bowls. They pieced together stained glass.

"Glass!" thought Octavio. "El vidrio es asombroso!"

By 15 years of age he was working in this glass shop, helping the artisans. By 17 he was blowing glass and forming many of the products sold in the shop and other shops in the Gulf Coast cities.

"If you learn to play the piano," his father said, "you will always have a job."

"If you blow glass and make glass art," his mother said, "you will always have a job."

The father would shake his head.

With some years of hands-on labor, Octavio grew to be a stout, young man with much muscle, the sweat from the heaters and ovens seemingly squeezing off any fat from his body.

At 22 years old, Octavio read that a man named Michael Owens engineered the first automatic bottle blowing machine that could now produce millions of light bulbs a day. The newspaper almost fell out of Octavio's hands. One…million…a…day! Factories were already making thousands of soda bottles. He took his tacos and his glass bottle of cola and walked to the beach. The art invented by the Syrians in the first century BC, was now being replaced by machines. Since that day, he lost most of his love for the process and just considered it all just hot, hard, monotonous work. A job.

Day after day, the sweat drained his heart. The heat cooked his constitution into a tar-like skin. The owner eventually died of some cancer. His father died. The woman he loved did not want to marry him. And then, the Revolution… talk of the Revolution was in the air more and more. There were so many wrongs with the Mexican government. So many strange things happening but not around him, because the coast was a happy place and people lived as well as they could there. But he read and heard of the stories of others. The slavery, the starvation. No jobs. The crimes of the municipalities. The states.

Zapata. Villa! He joined the Revolution. He was assigned to the army of Generalissimo Pancho Villa. His hands lost the touch of glass and became the hands of a soldier. A killer. And, in some times he thought, the paws of an animal. A criminal too, for the war was like a murky piece of blurry, brown glass. Stained with dried blood, not once in beautiful colors.

When the men of his unit rode into the cattle ranch this day, and the man with the bullwhip shot his Colonel Octavio, he wanted to stay. Stay and shoot all the men who challenged them, challenged the Revolution. But his horse turned away suddenly with all the other horses, and ran to escape the flying bullets. To stay there in the front yard, meant to stay and shoot, and to die almost alone.

Now he was escaping with these men, but like scared children? From only a handful of men chasing them?

"NO!" he thought. "No more."

"Para, pelea!" he yelled. Stop and fight!

But no one did. So, he did. He stopped his horse and leaped from her. In the ways of the cavalry, Octavio twisted the horse's head and neck, causing her to lie flat. She was a trained horse, but the fleeing action of the herd for the moment, took her mind from her work and she resisted this suicidal tactic. He won, and she laid flat. He pulled the rifle from the saddle scabbard and dropped down behind her to shoot. His beautiful horse, his pet, was now his shield. He aimed the rifle at the charging men and fired.

He must have missed. He worked the lever action and… then a bullet tore through his talented left hand, the one he once used to tap such tunes across the piano keys of his grandmother's piano, and spin the pipe and blow tons of such magical glass and prisms of glorious colors. He had but one confused second to look at this hand, feel the burn on it like a careless mistake back at the glass shop, when another bullet struck and shattered his forehead. He convulsed, gagged and instantly died. Both bullets came from the pistol of Bullwhip Pierce. The horse wrestled itself afoot, but did not run. It stood still by its master, smelling his face.

Bullwhip and the pursuers ran right past the body of Octavio Histafa and the big mistake that was once his life.

Chapter 14: Day of the The Himalaya Breakfast Burrito

"Hello!" Venzula said loudly as he stepped inside the gun store. "Buenas dias!"

His group of dusty, big-hatted men, all smiling, filed in slowly behind him, looking around, trying to appear like casual shoppers.

"It seems that there is a big interest in shotguns today," Venzula said, eyeing the guns next to everyone in the shop. This quick observation was not good news for the holders of this little Alamo. But his little contingent had not caught on to his English comments.

Suddenly, a teenager, Georgie Potter from the Hamhocks Restaurant appeared in the door, wearing a white shirt, jeans and apron, weaving his way through the men. He looked up at Hercules high in his corner nest, and noticed the giant man's table was turned over. Only the top of his head appeared over the edge and he had the eyes of a demon.

"Hima...Himalaya?" Georgie said sheepishly, with curious raised eyebrows and voice, holding the food bag up. It was time for Hercules' daily, morning Himalaya breakfast burrito delivery.

Mellencholly strummed the guitar softly off to the left -

"It's only you my darling," Mellencholly sang.

"It's only you my love.

It's through heaven I have found you.

It's through heaven I've found love..."

Venzula smiled at the burrito problem.

Hercules said nothing. He did try to nudge his head to the side to suggest Georgie move over, or even leave.

"No. No breakfast today, Georgie," Chueng said. "Best you...."

"Himalaya!" Venzula said. "Burrito! Perhaps I should eat this then, if no one else will?"

Venzula slowly reached out for the boy. But the reach was a bit unnatural and not just for the bag of food, rather it was to scoop the boy up as a shield with his left hand. His right hand rose to get his holstered gun.

"Now!" Gunther yelled.

The store literally exploded with the gunfire of many calibers in the first devastating wave unleashed by the store defenders.

The soldiers didn't have guns drawns, nor were they expecting much resistance this morning, nor could they follow the conversation in English that prompted the battle.

Hercules raked his pump shotgun rounds at the men below him by the front doors, trying not to hit the poor boy.

Glass counters and windows shattered.

Gunther shot who he could still see. When a handgun ran empty he pulled another of his five weapons.

Wood splintered.

Mellencholly dropped to the floor and from his angle of vision, shot the men by the front door.

Men screamed, hollered, cursed.

Selleck dropped to a knee and shot who he could see down the end of his aisle.

Gunsmoke filled the air.

Chueng and his employees shot wildly in the general directions of the invaders.

No one could shoot right at Venzula. He was low and behind layers of his chaotic men. Venzula did shoot back randomly at Gunther, Chueng and Sampson, but crouched, he hauled Georgie behind the soldiers and dashed out of the store.

The gunfire subsided, only the sounds of coughs, moans and gags remained.

"Whose hurt?" Gunther shouted as he stepped forward to the door.

"Not me," Mellencholly said.

"Nor me," said Selleck.

"I...none...none of us," Chueng said.

Gunther marched to the door. He saw a few of the soldiers still alive, still fumbling for their pistols. Gunther shot each one in the head as he went by. He stopped by the wall near the doors and reloaded his pistols.

"Georgie?" Hercules yelled from his nest.

"He's okay," Gunther said, looking outside while reloading.

Georgie Potter was on the sidewalk, sitting up, leaning on one skinny arm.

"Venzula is out of sight," Gunther said, carefully stepping from window to window. "He musta' pitched the kid down and ran."

Gunther opened one of the splintered doors, now just a open wooden and metal frame.

"Georgie! Get in here! Come on," Gunther yelled.

The kid got up and ran for the store as Gunther watched over him. He passed Gunther and stopped at the lobby, shocked at the human, mashed, bloody rubble.

"Go on up there with Hercules," Gunther told him. "Go on."

"Well, dammit!" Mellencholly shouted.

Everyone looked his way, fearing the worst.

"My guitar's shot up."

"Mister Mellencholly," Chueng said, "you can have any guitar in this place."

Selleck walked to the front lobby, confirming that everyone was properly dead.

"They barely got a shot off," Selleck said. "They weren't ready for us."

"Mr Selleck," Chueng asked. "Would you like anything?"

"I do believe, I would like...to leave. I have had my fill of all things gun today, Mr Chueng," he said. "And, as I am no musician, no instruments. But, I would like to know what in Hell is going on."

"Pancho Villa is here recruiting mercenaries," Gunther said, while separating the dead from their guns. "And often when he is done in a town, he rapes the whole place."

"I've picked a terrible time to go shopping, haven't I?" Selleck said, wiping his brow with his sleeve.

"So did I," Gunther looked up at him and said with a woeful expression.

"How's about this en here?" Mellencholly said, holding up a guitar.

"Please, sir, it is yours," Chueng said.

"If you gentlemen don't mind, since I was just passing though, I think I will...pass through," Selleck said. He stepped and hopped over the dead to the front door. "I don't want to hang around to take on the rest of an army."

"I understand, sir," Gunther said. "I wish I could leave." He stood up from his weapon search. "But I've had two teenage boys in my charge, now dead because of them. Just this morning. And there will be a reckoning."

"This here was quite a reckoning, Mr Gunther."

"Not enough of one."

Selleck raised his bushy eyebrows. He got to the front doors, and turned, smiled and waved goodbye.

"God bless you, sir," Chueng said.

"Me too," Mellencholly said. "See ya at Christmas." He walked to the doors with his new instrument. Then he turned and smiled and said, "Just kidding', I ain't a coming back here. This is about the craziest guitar store I've ever been in."

"Hold on!" Chueng said.

Chueng grabbed a black guitar case, hustled around the corner of a shattered counter and marched up to Mellencholly.

"Here sir, you need this too." He handed him the case.

"Yes, I do." And he left the store behind Selleck. They all watched as both men carefully walked outside and rounded the corner. They appeared again, Selleck in a small, single horse carriage and Mellencholly on a horse. They waved to each other and went their separate ways.

Gunther and Chueng then examined the shop. Their end of the store was a disaster.

"They never knew, we knew, they were coming," Chueng said.

"Yup."

"Wow."

"We ambushed the ambush," Gunther said. "I'll bet they're not used to be being challenged. Look, some may come back later," Gunther said. "Get your doorman here right away. Call the Marshal's Office and tell them what happened. Maybe they can spare a few folks. Load up. Stand guard."

He looked outside at the Mexican ponies. "Seems to me you just got yourself about 10 some odd horses."

"Seems so. And a whole lot of guns too." He pushed some pistols around with his boot, looking them over. What are you going to do?" Chueng asked.

"I'm going to see what else I can do around here," Gunther said.

"Reckoning," Chueng said.

"Reckoning," Gunther repeated.

On the corner platform, Hercules looked the grocery store boy over. His shirt was splashed with blood, but he was alright. Georgie handed him the Himalaya burrito bag, that he never once dropped through the whole melee!

Hercules smiled, unwrapped the burrito and took a big bite. Chueng saw this and grabbed the handle of the metal coffee pot behind the counter. He was shaking bad enough to almost slosh the coffee out of it. He set it back down, took a deep breath, steadied himself and poured a cup. He reached up and handed the cup to giant buddy.

The front door, security man finally showed up for work in his clean, pressed suit. He was busy looking at the pack of horses outside, went to push on the front door glass to enter and found only..."air." Glass gone.

"What happened here?"

"Gunther stepped through an empty door frame rather than open the door. He wanted to say something, took a breath to start, but shook his head and let the moment pass.

Chapter 15: Mexican Stand-Off
August 1924 Omaha, Nebraska

"Go on," Lt. Hawes said.

"Well, sir," Calabash said, "Gunther suggested I get down
to the Marshal's Office and help out. It's downright funny, ya
know because I went to Tremboro to join the Revolution and
I wound up fighting against it. I asked somebody where the
police station was and they told me. It was a big, new place,
and I walked in. There was a bunch of men in there and some
women. They all had guns and bags of who knows what all.
Ammo? Lunch? Some was wearing badges and some was
not. A deputy was givin' out orders and telling people where
to go in town.

The deputy asked me who I was, and I told em. I told em I
was there to hep out. He waved his hand around in front of
me like a Catholic preacher and declared I was now a deputy
in and of the posse. I said fine. Fine. The Marshal got close,
handed me a silver badge and said that the mercury mine up
in the hills had a little police force. Like guards. And that we
needed to ride up there to make sure they were okay and they
didn't get themselves robbed or kilt."

"Where was Gunther at this time?" Pershing asked.

"Well, I found out later he was just finishing up a helluva' gunfight at the gun store. They got a few of us some horses, what needed them, and about 15 of us, the Marshal included, took off for the mines. But...we soon rode right straight into a mess on the steps of the national bank..."

****

October 1915, Tremboro, Texas

"Stop! Stop!" The bald witch yelled.

Jefe did not stop Black Magic as Celesta jogged beside him. He scanned the streets ahead. The city looked deserted. And he could hear bursts of gunfire here and there in the distance. Things were falling apart. Breaking down.

"Felix Jefe Cocoy!" she screamed in Spanish. "Stop!"

Jefe pulled back on the reins of Black Magic. He turned to her.

"How in de world, do you know my full name?" he said in Spanish.

She stared at him, with such an odd face, suggesting that she didn't know how she knew either.

"I know your name from your trips here."

"No you don't."

"Listen to me," she said. "I need to lay down a bad prayer, a spell on Pancho Villa. A spell."

The horse's head seemed to bolt up a bit at the mention of Villa.

"But I need to have some metal that he has touched. The bastard! I need metal for the spell."

"Spell," Jefe said with a half-smiled. "Kulam. Pagkuku-lam. This is the black magic of the Philippines." He looked away from her to again scan the streets.

"It is the same. It is all the same," she said. "The powers. You know the powers. The powers at work underneath all of this."

Page 160

Jefe stared ahead. An educated man. College educated in Spain. But the culture of his villages, his islands, ran deep. And there were so many unanswerable questions about the world. The realms of faith. The realms of magic.

"I was just told at the stables, that Pancho Villa played golf this morning," Jefe said.

"Yes?"

"He must of used golf clubs."

"Yes," she said.

"I will feel of those golf clubs." She put her hand on his knee. "We will have this day, senor," she said, and sprinted down the street.

Jefe then heard some loud thumps and bangs from around the corner, and then some loud orders in Spanish. And the words "Open up!" in English. He turned Black Magic's head and touched his right heel to the horse's flank to walk on and to see the source. The streets were all paved in this area of downtown and the horse shoes clopped heavily upon it.

Right at the turn now in Jefe's view, sat the Tremboro National Bank. Ten revolutionaries lingered on the stone steps and sidewalk of the establishment. Some on horses. Some afoot. Some banging on the main double doors, and banging on the windows, cursing. The window had bars over them. Inside each window were clay skull decorations for the Day of the Dead. Jefe was suddenly too close to them to back away.

"Hey you!" one soldado said to Jefe. "Hey, what time does this bank open up?"

Jefe shrugged his shoulders.

"De sign says 9 a.m. It is after 9!" another said.

"Maybe it is closed today?" Jefe said in Spanish.

"Naaaah, hey wait a moment," a man by the door said. Jefe spotted military rank stitched on the man's dusty jacket.

"I know you. And, I know this horse."

"That is the horse of Venzula," another soldier said.

And with that, almost all the men walked toward Jefe. Jefe remained stoic. They surrounded him, looking him over.

"These are very nice guns you have, senor."

And this horse...Colonel Venzula would like, very much, to have this horse back, I think," said another.

"Very nice pistols..."

"This horse," Jefe said calmly in Spanish, "belongs to my partner, Johann Gunther, who bought the horse from Colonel Venzula for a handsome price only yesterday. Gunther and I have joined de Revolution this morning, as Generalissimo Villa has requested us, after we had dinner with him last night. We are leaving with your army today, and I am going to find Gunther right now so we can leave. We will fight for the Revolution."

The men stared at Jefe.

"Oh," said a soldier.

"So, you can see, my new friends, I need my guns and my horse to help you fight."

"Oh," said another.

"Yes. I saw you at the cantina last night," yet another one said.

The men seemed disappointed and backed away. A soldado started kicking on the bank doors, and everyone's attention turned back to the bank. Then two more men joined in with the kicking. The doors were sturdy and not giving an inch.

"I have visited this city before," Jefe shouted. "I have been to this bank as we have bought guns here before. Even if you break the doors down, the safe is very big and heavy. Very thick. You cannot break into it. And you cannot move it."

"We are ordered to get money from this bank, for the Revolution," a soldier told Jefe.

"I understand, but without any employees here to threaten, you can do nothing."

"Do you know where the president of the bank is?" one asked.

"No."

A rolling thunder of hooves on payment grew louder. Jefe backed Black Magic up to see who was coming. When he saw Marshal Heston and Calabash, with deputies and volunteers, some dozen men, he was relieved and continued backing up from the soldiers. The lawmen rounded the corner and stopped before the bank.

"It would seem, sir," Jefe said to the marshal, "these men wish to break into the bank."

No guns were out, no guns were pointed yet.

"Nooooo, no," the leader said with a smile. "We were ordered by Generalissimo Pancho Villa to axe de presidentay of de bank for a donation for de cause of de Revolution."

Jefe, ever the flanker, slowly moved to the right. He turned Black Magic to face the side of the Mexicans. Calabash saw this and slowly joined him.

"The bank is closed," the marshal said sternly.

"Closed?"

"Closed."

"Can you, can you find de presidentay so we can axe him for help? Por favor?"

"No."

"No?" Heston said.

"No."

"What if..." the leader said, "what if...." and he suddenly yanked out his pistol in a blur, and pointed it at the Marshal. "What if I ask your men to find de presidentay or, or...I will shoot the Marshal of dis village? Huh? Can we *now* find de presidentay?"

"No," Heston said calmly.

All the men of the posse, either lifted their rifles or pulled their pistols out and aimed at the leader. Jefe had both his pistols out, Calabash his. This sudden hostage attempt was fast and a surprise to his own soldiers, and none of them drew their weapons. They just stood there watching.

"The bank is closed, Sergeant," the Marshal said again sternly.

"The president ain't coming. And you are about to be blown to smithereens if you don't put that pistol down. So, do it."

The leader made a sad face, then burst out in forced laughter. He put the pistol back into his holster. He looked at his men. Some laughed with him also. Some...did not.

"Geet' outta' here," the marshal growled.

The posse backed up as the soldados got on their horses. They started to leave.

"You! You! Hahhhaha," the leader said with a big, laughing grin as he passed the marshal. "You know, I was just joking at you."

"I hope you men win the Revolution," the marshal said. And he meant it.

"Good luck," another Tremboro man added.

"Yeah," said another.

"And you!" the leader pointed at Jefe. "You are a very clever man, senor," he said in Spanish. "I am to guess, you did *not* join de Revolution."

Jefe said nothing and watched them leave.

"Viva da le Revolution!" some of the men shouted. Some of the soldiers even smiled at them and some waved goodbye.

Calabash wrinkled up his face, took off his hat and rubbed his head with a big sigh.

"Was that what they call a...Mexican Stand-off?"

"That...I believe my friend, was a very, very real, Mexican Stand-off," Felix Jefe Oscar said.

Chapter 16: Chase of the Kidnappers

Chueng's store looked like a cattle ranch, butcher shop. Gunther couldn't waste time with the bodies on the floor, hauling them out into the street, and washing the floors on hands and knees as the employees needed to do. He knew he was needed elsewhere.

He walked cautiously out into the street. He looked up, down and all over for Venzula, but saw nothing. He climbed back into the auto after he started the engine and pulled onto the street from the parking lot, startling the Mexican horses. He had no destination in mind except perhaps the police station, or the telegraph office, anywhere he could receive reports of progress and go from there to help.

Then a thought struck him. The questions Villa was asking about the rich people and big houses. Chueng said that they lived on the north side of the city. With but a sketch of a map of Tremboro in his head, he turned north on the first main street he saw. Would Villa be there now? Orchestrating robberies? Kidnappings? Were Villa soldiers there now taking the houses apart, person by person? House to house? He raced north through the mostly deserted streets. Some men appeared at various street corners wearing stern faces, military and hunting rifles in their hands. Pistols hung on their hips. Some women of all ages were armed too. A number of Tremboro citizens had enough of waiting and cowering. Gunther tapped the car horn when he approached them, and they waved back.

He spotted one of the Mexican ambulances ahead, just parked on the street. He pulled up near the cab of the ambulance and could see the two medics inside, the same two he spoke to earlier about escaping, defecting from their new master.

"Hey!" Gunther shouted to them.

"Senor Gunther!" the driver said.

"Why are you just sitting here?"

"No one has told us to go anywhere," the driver said.

Gunther was stymied for a few seconds over that.

"And we are...how you say, hiding from Villa. We wish to go with you to San Antonio."

"Okay," Gunther said. "Well, follow me for now."

They started off, bound for that "rich" housing edition. With the car top still down, he could see the whole area clearly. An exit north of him appeared that led to a stately collection of homes to the east. The housing edition sat on a coveted rise of the land. No fires. No gunshots. No war that he could see or hear.

He turned right, onto this last, long road east to the houses with the ambulance behind him. It was still all quiet up ahead, until...until something did emerge on the road. Moving dots. A cluster of horsemen at a trot. What...?

They grew closer. The big hats. The bandoleers on the torsos. Six soldiers were riding closer... wait...seven horsemen. Wait. Gunther stared in deeper. There was a woman riding the middle horse, in between them all. Blonde hair. Not a woman...it was a teenage girl.

As they drew closer, Gunther could spy that the teenager's mouth was wrapped by a strip of cloth, her hands were tied to the saddle horn and one soldier was holding the lead rope of her horse. She was a prisoner!

They were soon to pass each other! Gunther put on a great,

big smile. As the unit approached, he waved at the men. The girls eyes were wide and her head shook like she was screaming for his attention. Two of the soldados waved back at him, perhaps recognizing him from the dinner the night before? And, the friendly man in the car was being followed by their ambulance. Perhaps another Villa mission? No doubt, they waved to the men in the ambulance behind him.

Gunther made it to the first intersection and turned the auto around. Then he gassed the car back west. He passed the ambulance and the curious faces of the medics and he made a circular motion in the air with his hand to follow him around too.

He drove closer and closer to the back side of the riders. Back in his cavalry days, he was taught by an old army trainer, that when chasing bandits or Indians, whether in a hot pursuit or sneaking up on them, if you could shoot the ones in the front and slow the enemy down. Or, if your plan was to surprise, shoot, pick off the ones in the rear, instead. Sometimes the leaders up front didn't know about the rear guard attrition. Gunther knew such plans were situational. And this might be such an odd situation. There was a girl in the middle that could be hit. The closer, rear men it was then!

The road was smooth. He grabbed a big revolver from the front seat next to him, stretched up a bit over the windshield and shot at the rearmost man. Based on the flutter of the rider's jacket and sudden shoulder shift, Gunther deduced he'd hit him. The man slowly slid off the horse and crashed onto the road, rolling like dead rubble, arms and legs spinning lifelessly. His horse though, kept moving with the pack. The body wound up off in the oncoming lane, no threat to Gunther's tires.

The men up ahead just kept their fast trotting pace! Was the clopping of horses' hooves on the pavement loud enough to cover his distant pistol shot? Gunther drove even closer. He took aim at the next rear man, but this one was not too far back from another rider and his loss might be detectable, the shot would probably not go unnoticed. Gunther took aim and fired again. Big sombreros shifted and the men turned fully to look back at him. They heard this one! The man in the rear fell off the back of his horse too. The remaining four men seemed confused now, stretching and craning their necks to look around. They took off at a dead run. This time, Gunther had to swerve hard not to hit his latest victim laying prone on the avenue.

Car verus horse. Mechanical "horse" power. Gunther attended a race back in Fort Worth a few years earlier. A 1914 Packard ran 70 miles an hour, versus a horse which was clocked at 35 miles per hour. But the horse could not keep up the pace for too long.

Gunther drove closer and closer. The rear horseman over to the left of the group tried to turn around, pistol in his right hand to shoot back at him, but Gunther veered way off to the left. The rider couldn't turn that far round in the saddle. Then the horseman to the right tried the same trick and shot, but Gunther stayed to the left. If they'd just continued to take turns like this, Gunther thought he could outlast them, swerve by swerve.

The horses spread apart preventing him from driving beside them, either by design or unintentionally. He drove up almost to the rear of the girl's horse, stood up a bit behind the wheel again, and shot the rider ahead of him and to the left. Twice. That rider also fell off the horse. Now the man holding the girl's lead rope was gone! Gunther pulled up a bit more to see that her hands were tied close down on the saddle horn. She could barely reach the lower end of the horse's mane for steerage, but she tried and obviously a good rider, she was working in the saddle with her knees and feet in the stirrups to slow the horse down, but it still wanted to run with its pack.

Two riders left. One up front and one to the right. Gunther could shoot....but the rider to the right suddenly stopped in a great display of horsemanship. The horse bucked and nayed, but stopped. The rider instantly vanished behind him.

"Damn!" Gunther cursed. An armed problem now to his rear. He ducked low.

Over his engine noise he could hear a few shots from that rider behind them. The soldado had to realize he was risking shooting his new kidnap victim as well as the front running amigo by just throwing shots up the road at Gunther. But if he was really angry enough, maybe it didn't matter to him?

Distance was their friend for the moment and Gunther let the rider, the victim, and car blow down the road. Gunther drove up to the victim on her right side. She was struggling with her binding. She looked at him with desperation. He took the Bowie knife in his left hand from his belt, leaned far over to her and tried to get near the horn on that saddle with his knife. Car and saddle horn were about the same height. The rider up front tried to peek back at them. He stretched and reached...

She put her hands as low as she could go on either side of the horn. The horse swerved. The car swerved just as Gunther tried to make a slash at the horn and not chop a body part off! Once. Twice. Misses. The hard left turn for downtown rapidly approached.

Another swing. The knife hit the wooden horn of the Mexican saddle. It splintered the rope. The teenager was able to unhook it. She leaned forward like a racer and got her hands into the horses mane.

The lead rider slowed for the sharp turn ahead. The teen proved she was indeed quite a rider, and she turned right to escape. Gunther hit the brakes to turn south. He skidded south around the corner. He grabbed a lever action rifle from the passenger seat, pulled on the brake stopping the car in another skid. Handbrake on. He jumped to the right side of the vehicle. He laid the rifle on the hood, took aim at the fleeing man and shot with just a little lead, knocking him right off the horse.

Bam! Bam! In from the left!

That rider once behind him was still charging forward, shooting bullets from his pistola in a flinging motion. The car windshield burst. He heard the harsh metallic thuds of rounds hitting the side of the car.

Gunther spun his rifle around and poured three rifle rounds at the rider, hitting him in the torso in two separate spots and the third right in the thigh. His leg blew back and this kicked him off the back of the steed. The horse did slow down and, like all the others, it just ran off.

Gunther lowered his rifle, took a deep breath and surveyed all the men. Were they all dead? The ambulance, that had u-turned behind him before the chase was now slowly heading his way,
driving around the downed men, ignoring their medical conditions. He stepped out onto the open road. He whistled and waved at the ambulance, hat in one hand, rifle in the other. It sped his way.

Then the teenager galloped up to him.

"Thank you, thank you, sir," she said.

"Are you alright?" Gunther asked.

"They kidnapped me. They kidnapped me." She jumped off the horse.

"Uh-huh."

"They broke into my house, they tied up my mom and dad and...my brother...and they took me. They took money and told my dad that he would hear from them, through El Paso newspapers and he would have to pay more money to get me back."

She hugged Gunther.

"You are lucky," he said.

"How did you know to come and rescue me?"

"I knew there would probably be kidnappings out this way, and I came to stop them."

The ambulance pulled up.

"What's your name?" Gunther asked.

"Melissa Mellbury."

"Very nice to meet you, Melissa."

The ambulance drivers got out of the big van and ran up to them.

"Can you take Melissa back to her house and help untie her family?" Gunther asked. "Make sure everyone is alright?"

"Si senor. What of these men that are shot."

"You can leave those sorry sons a bitches," Gunther said. "I think they're dead anyway. Take care of her and her family then get to the police station downtown. Help anyone there you can. I will see you there."

"You can trust them," Gunther said, turning to the girl. "They were kidnapped too. And they have made a deal with me."

They started to guide her to the vehicle.

"What...wait...what is your name?" she asked.

"Gunth..." he reached into his pocket, took out his wallet and pulled out a card. "Johann Gunther, Remedies Investigation, Fort Worth, Texas."

He got back into the car, pulled off the hand brake and drove back to downtown Tremboro. He passed the dead man's horse along the way. It had slowed to a trot and gave him a quick look as he drove by.

Chapter 17: Return of the Poison Pill
August 1924, Omaha, Nebraska

"The ride up to the mining company took about 20 minutes at a healthy horse trot," Calabash told the Army interviewers. "But Jefe galloped Black Magic on ahead, like a volunteer scout. That feller is somethin' else. He's a soldier and well, I'll tell ya why in a minute. There was a slow incline and some twists and turns to the trail. Off to the left was an unfinished railroad I guess to haul the mercury to the station faster. Pretty soon we saw Jefe again when we got close. He was still mounted, looking at the mining company from a short distance aways. The mine had a wooden fence around it. Lots of wooden buildings and big office looking building, best we could see. Jefe galloped back to us, with a mighty sour face. And what he saw, what we saw next was a fuse to a nightmare. The Marshal held the matchstick..."

****

October 1915, Tremboro, Texas

"I'll go," Jefe offered. "I was a scout in the Army."

"Okay," the Marshal said.

With 10 minutes Jefe returned with the intelligence.

"The mining guards are all sitting on the ground," Jefe told the Marshal and the posse. "No guns. They've surrendered. The workers are standing or sitting too. Villa soldiers are standing guard. The guards look toward the office a lot. Watching. Waiting. Something must be going on in there."

Marshal Heston nodded. All eyes were on the distant mining grounds. Two men had binoculars and one had a telescope. They studied the problem.

"How many you reckon?" the marshal asked.

"Fourteen soldiers men," Jefe said. "Twenty-one horses."

"Seven inside. Seven..."

"What are we gonna' do, Marshal?" a deputy interrupted.

"We have 14 here," he said.

They all sat on their horses quietly.

"Well shit," the Marshal said. "We can't *not*...go in. We... are here." He turned his horse to face the posse.

"Anyone here wants to leave, I mean, I won't hold it against ya. Ya didn't sign on to raid some kind of ...fort..." he pointed a thumb over his shoulder to the camp, "...held by a bunch of damn Mexican soldiers. This ain't law enforcement no more. This is...a small war."

Everyone sat still. One horse snorted.

"We're...with...ya...Marshal," one volunteer said, but there was a definite tone of regret.

"You?" the Marshal jutted his long jaw out at Jefe. "Yer not even from around here."

"I'm with you," Jefe said.

"You?" the Marshal asked Calabash. "You came here to be one of them, didn't you?"

"Now I'm with him," Calabash said, as he raised a finger from his saddle horn grasp to point at Jefe. "He's with you and I'm with you. Sure, I'm with ya. Ya showed a lotta lead in yer balls back at the bank."

"So be it," one of the men said.

"Thank you," another said.

"We have to see this through," said another.

"Okay. Okay, here's what I'm thinking," the Marshal said, "we're gonna ride in slow. Ride right up to the office. You four men stay back by the gate. Just inside the gate. The rest of us ride in. I'm gonna dismount and walk into the office and see what the hell's going on. Like nothing is going on. Just slow-ride up and walk in."

"I'll go in with you," Jefe said.

"I can't ask..."

"I will go in with you."

"Okay, Mister Jefe."

"I'll go in too," Calabash said.

The Marshal looked back at him, a bit shocked.

"You said it's a war," Calabash said. "I was a soldier once and Jefe was an officer in the army. We'll be going in there with ya, Marshal."

Calabash looked at the others, "You fellers been 'in'?"

They all shook their heads no to the military question.

"Well then," Calabash said, "we're a going in there, with ya."

"Okay," the Marshal said. "There's a big lobby and all the desks are right there. Even the manager's desk is right in the middle. Two big front doors. Several back doors. With all those men standing guard, we can't, not a one of us, sneak around and in the back."

"Front doors," Jefe said.

"Front doors," the Marshal said.

The lawman made a cricket sound with his mouth and his horse stepped off toward the business.

"Guns in the holsters. Rifles on yer laps," he said solemnly. "If there's shootin'? Duck and shoot the closest Villa son of bitch to you."

Jefe winked at Calabash. And they all rode off to this under-manned, under-gunned showdown.

They slow-walked into the mining compound through the open gateway. The soldiers remained still, watching them, their guns trained on the hostage, mining guards and the few workers caught out front when they arrived.

"Detener!" a sergeant yelled at them to stop.

But, they didn't stop. The posse took up the positions as first designed by Marshal Heston. They did not draw pistols or aim guns. They remained on their horses.

The Mexicans shifted their positions to cover these new arrivals.

"We are here to see your commander," Jefe told them in Spanish.

"Suelta tus armas!" the sergeant ordered.

"What he say?" Heston asked Jefe.

"He said to drop our guns."

"How do you say - that shit ain't a gonna happen in Spanish?" the Marshal said.

The Sergeant seemed very nervous. He knew he was on the edge of a bloodbath.

"We are here," Jefe repeated, "to see your commander, and we are going inside."

A few soldiers shouted something in Spanish, with the tone of orders, and with the tones of anger. The posse did not respond.

"These men do not speak Spanish," Jefe said to the soldiers, "so you can shout at them all you want, they will not understand you."

Jefe, the Marshal and Calabash dismounted calmly, as though they were walking into a restaurant for a meal. Two soldiers stood on either side of the big double doors of the stone and wood, office building.

"We are here only to speak with your commander," Jefe said to them, yet again in Spanish.

The duo remained at their posts.

Once inside they saw the scene. The front lobby was indeed huge and full of desks, chairs and tables. It had the look of big city office in Houston, or Dallas. At least 15 employees, men and women were there, dressed fashionably, standing throughout the room, staring at the center big desk, where the nightmare was talking place.

The nightmare was with the manager Jose Delarosa. He was seated and surrounded at his regal desk. One soldier had the manager's left arm pinned behind the back of his chair. Another soldier held the manager's right hand on the desk. A third soldier held the manager's head back by the forehead, with his head cranked over the back of the chair. The soldier's other hand held the manager's chin down and open. The manager's eyes were wide with fear. He was gagging. Sweating.

The commander, a colonel by uniform rank, held a silver spoon in his hand near the manager's face. Two soldiers with shotguns stood guard to the right and left of the desk.

Jefe could see into the silver spoon. It was that little ball of mercury Delarosa gave Villa the day before. The colonel waved the spoon an inch from the manager's forced open mouth.

"Buenas dias, Marshal," the colonel said, spotting the badge on the jacket. "Buenas dias." The colonel smiled. "Good that you can join us right now, Marshal. I am trying to get a donation for de Revolution from dis company. You know? But...dis man...he will not open up his heart! Open up his safe. And give us, just a little bit of money. Just a little. For dis bery, bery important cause. So, we open up his mouth until he opens the safe."

The colonel held a silver spoon in one hand, close to the manager's face.

Jefe slowly moved back. Calabash stepped to his right.

"What's that?" the marshal asked in a curious, yet still friendly tone. "Medicine? Er, poison medicine?"

"Dis? Dis is...a gift dis hombre gave to Generalissimo Pancho Villa yesterday. It is a little ball of mercury. You know, what dey make around here." He moved the spoon over to the marshal and lowered it. "You see? A little, little ball. Villa cannot accept dis gift of such a small ball, without a real donation to de Revolution. If we cannot get a donation? I must...you know...return dis gift? Pancho Villa *ordered* me to return dis gift." He turned his attention back to the manager's mouth, as though he were giving medicine to a child.

"Return it...as in his mouth," the marshal repeated.

"De mining of de mercury is good? Yes? Good business. Den we must have a good donation."

It was clear that the manager was so frightened, he could not speak.

"Agnes!" the Marshal shouted. "Open the safe!"

Agnes, stepped from the onlookers and nervously walked past them to a big, black and gold safe on the right wall.

"Ahhhh, AHA!" the colonel said. "It is bery good you are here, my amigo. I was glad to see you come in." He sat on the desk, next to the manager.

Agnes busied herself with the combination.

"We...we mean you no harm. We are here on de strictest of orders. To get donations, for de Revolution."

The colonel signaled for his shotgun guard to walk to the safe. The manager was still held tight in the man-made vice of revolutionaries.

Agnes stepped back. The soldier looked inside, turned back to the colonel and nodded.

The colonel nodded back. He turned to Delarosa.

"You see? We don't have to shoots no one here, we..." and then, clearly acting like a clumsy clown, *dropped* the little ball of mercury right into the manager's mouth.

"Oops," he said with smile, "I have made...."

And a bullet tore through the colonel's temple.

Jefe turned to see one of the workers in the lobby with a pistol, his arm stretched out full and face full of anger. He'd got a gun from somewhere when the guard walked off to the safe, and made the perfect shot, some 20 feet away to the colonel's head, and this war was on.

Jefe immediately pulled both his pistols and shot the closest guard next to him in the head, chest and throat with his left gun, and riddled the man to the left of Delarosa's chair with his right gun.

The armed employee fired and fired at the soldier by the safe. Agnes dove for cover, as did everyone else. The wounded soldier shot back as he too jumped aside and limped for the back of the office.

Calabash ran for the back of the room too, hitting the soldier behind the chair twice with Colt .45 rounds, then he pelted four more at the soldier limping across the room.

Shotgun pellets tore open the marshal's left arm and shoulder, but he still pulled and shot the charging shotgunner.

Between the Marshal and Calabash, they put the man down as he crashed lifeless into the furniture.

The two door guards turned in from the open doors, as Jefe expected. The marshal dropped to the floor and fired. Calabash was behind the manager's desk. They shot at the doormen, as Jefe dashed at them from the side, firing both guns. All the rounds, some 14 bullets cut through the air and cut the guards down like they were struck by lightening. Even that impulsive salesman helped.

Jefe said, "Whose got rounds in their guns?" Jefe asked.

"I do," the Marshal said.

"Watch the front doors. Everyone else reload. Now." Then, Jefe said to the office group, "If any of you have a gun here? Get it. Otherwise get their guns. Is there medical staff here?"

"Yes," a woman replied.

"Get them," he said, "your manager needs to vomit."

Silence.

Silence outside too? The officer workers picked up the guns off the floor. The ones with guns in their desks pulled their's out. Agnes grabbed a shotgun from the dead man in the clutter of furniture and walked sternly to near the side of the front door.

Jefe peeked out a window. It seemed like the soldiers and the posse outside were just waiting to see what happened inside. Perhaps each side thought their party inside had won? That their colonel had killed the visitors?

Another man and woman laid the manager, chest down, on his desk, with his upper torso and head hanging down off the end. They began pounding his back. He coughed and gagged.

Two salesmen dashed to the marshal and stood him up so he could lean on the desk. Once up, Heston brushed them off as though he was okay, but he was not. His prior fall to the floor was not a tactical move, even though he shot well from that position. They examined his shoulder wounds. Calabash put bullets in his gun and walked up to the Filipino. Jefe visually checked over the office. He nodded to the Heston and the

Marshal started to reload. Everyone seemed to be as ready as they were going to get, a few armed with office pistols, varment rifles and some of their own personal pistols.

The Marshal took a giant breath, straightened his back and walked up to Jefe.

"Get another pistol," Jefe told Calabash and the Marshal, as they only had one gun each. They turned their heads to look for one, some employees handed each a second gun taken from the dead men.

"Loaded?" Jefe asked.

"Loaded," the Marshal checked and said.

"Loaded," Calabash checked and said.

"Let me talk,"Jefe said. "I speak Spanish." He walked out, two pistols pointed down, the Marshal to the left. Calabash to the right of him. Even Agnes, armed with a shotgun, stepped out on the porch. All eyes were on them.

"Who is in charge out here?" Jefe asked in Spanish.

The men looked at each other and the sergeant who first confronted them, looked around at his comrades, stepped forward and answered.

"I am. Sergeant Jose Ajuntas."

"Your colonel is dead," Jefe said in Spanish. "And the men with him. They were torturing the manager here. Breaking the American law. Inside we now have many people with guns. We have many people with guns out here. Your mission to get money from here has failed. We can all die here today for nothing, or, Sgt. Ajuntas, you can lead your men away, back to Mexico and fight in the Revolution. You have no Revolution to fight here in Texas. There is no reason to die here today, for a crime, like a criminal, like an armed bandido, not a soldier. In Texas, we in Texas support your Revolution. We wish you well. Just leave us alone."

Silence.

But the silence was broken with the sounds of loud vomiting from inside.

Sgt. Ajuntas walked up to the steps of the balcony.

"May we recover the body of the colonel?" he asked Jefe.

"Of course. Wait."

Jefe shouted to the men inside to produce the body. Within a moment three salesmen appeared on the porch with the heavy corpse. They carried the colonel down the steps and laid him on the cobblestone walkway.

Marshal Heston staggered a little. Jefe spotted the blood stain on his shirt grow.

Some of the soldiers took the dead man. They carried him over to a magnificent, looking horse and hefted the body over the saddle.

"Amigos," Sgt. Ajuntas said in Spanish. "Mount up. We go."

The posse made space at the entrance. The unit got on their horses. And they slowly left the enclosed grounds. The posse dismounted, but Jefe stopped two of them.

"Follow them a bit, from a distance. Shoot twice in de air, if they turn back," Jefe told them. "They lost a lot today and someone might get crazy mad and come back."

Jefe watched them all leave.

"Pancho Villa," Jefe said, "is a very bad model as a leader. He tortures and kills. He teaches his men to be sly and tricky and is quick to do the same." He looked inside the office doors and shouted in, "We need help for the Marshal."

The Marshal stared at Jefe's profile.

"Who...who in hell are you anyway?" he asked.

"Felix Jefe Cocoy," he said.

"All the way from the Philippines?"

"All the way."

"I don't know how in the hell you got here, Mister Jefe, but I'm sure glad you did."

Jefe got under the tall man's arm and helped him inside.

The guards and workers ran up the steps and back inside the office to help.

"Yer salesman here is a real hero!" Calabash told them, pointing at the man who shot the colonel in the head. "What's yer' name sir?"

"Julio Regard," the man said. "but, I think I almost got

us...all kilt",'' the man admitted. He sat on a desk and laid his
pistol down beside him.

"You did the right thing, Julio," the Marshal said, avoiding the manager's vomit on the floor in front of the big desk.
Jefe sat him in a chair on the side of the manager's desk. A
man and a woman took off his shirt and tended to the wound.
Jefe took a look. He made a head motion side-to-side and an
expression as if the wound wasn't *too* bad.

"Not sure I can ride back," Heston told Jefe with a gasp.

"We've got a automobile to getcha' back, Marshal," a
salesman said.

"Marshal!" a deputy yelled as he bounded into the office,
"You alright?"

"I'm alright, Smitty," Heston said. "Tell everyone we are
alright. I am the only damn fool to get shot in this fracas." He
looked at Agnes.

"Agnes, will you call the police station and tell them what
happened."

"Tell em to tell my wife I am okay too!" Deputy Smitty
blurted out to her, then looked a little sheepish.

"Welllll, looky' here, looky here," Calabash said, standing
over the vomit. "Right there. Look. There's that little ball of
black magic *piiison* right there. See it?"

Jefe stepped over and looked down at the bauble of mercury.

The Manager Delarosa was in another chair to the side,
and looked like six kinds of hell. With his legs spread apart in
the chair, everyone could see he'd peed his pants.

"Not to worry, senor," Calabash said to him. "That little
pill didn't open up er nothin' when inside ya' gut. You hacked
it all up. In its *entirety*."

Delarosa moaned.

Chapter 18: Singing Songs at Christmas

Venzula fled the gun store and met up with two of his compadres. He had one last mission for Villa before they could leave Tremboro and run back across the Rio Grande border. One soldier with him was the sad hombre in the maroon sombrero who fell prey to the whip and bolo test the day before. The other was a veteran soldier with Venzula for two years.

Venzula knew he failed badly at the gun store. There was no ambush *of* the store as he had planned. Just an ambush *on them*. Damn that Gunther. How did he know? Venzula knew he was lucky to escape by charging low behind his men for cover and leaping out the door. Unscathed. He hoped that their other units were successful in their raids at the ranch, the mine and the bank. If he could at least get Villa that bag of golf clubs he wanted, the set he had used earlier that morning, he would be somewhat vindicated by showing support for Villa's new hobby. One never knew how Villa would react to a failure, a success or a gift.

In the abandoned Tremboro town center, the three men sat on horseback. Venzula studied a crudely hand drawn, city map.

"We go that way," he pointed, and they spurred their horses east. Venzula had a personal quest of his own, too. A human one. A bloodthirsty one.

Tremboro was now mostly a ghost town. Though some congregated on corners and under the awnings of some businesses, most residents peeked out of dark and shaded windows as the three horsemen trotted by. They received investigative stares, grimaces and even some threats.

"Get out of here!"

"Get out and stay out!"

"Keep moving."

The man in the maroon sombrero was very nervous. Venzula was not. The three men lumbered along, looking as unthreatening as possible. Venzula often waved and smiled at them. Sometimes some of the small groups would step out into street as the three passed. Occasional bursts of gunfire still pounded off in the

distance from different calibers of firearms.

Gunther drove into Tremboro proper, bound for the police station. But, he suddenly felt sick. Confused thoughts. Dizzy. Dizzy-sick like he felt hours earlier in his hotel room. He pulled over to the sidewalk and parked. He rubbed his head. What was this? He'd never experienced a sickness like this after any violence. Maybe from the death of those boys? Yes, maybe, was it all catching up with him? But, this was a weird, floating feeling like back in the hotel room. His head just slumped down. He stared at his hands laying on his lap. He drooled a bit from his open mouth.

He closed his eyes and opened them and a golf club appeared in his hands, laying across his thighs. What? He blinked. Shook his head. Looked at his hands again. They were empty. Lap empty. The golf club was gone. What was that? He didn't feel anything in his hands, yet he saw the club in his hands. He looked around the front seat of the automobile. There were no golf clubs! Never had been. He rubbed his eyes again. He swore he saw a golf club in his hands. A paper skeleton blew across the street in front of him. It rolled over the hood of the car and hooked on the windshield frame. Glass gone, its simplistic skeleton face sort of mocked him. He reached over and tore the figure from the car, and it flew away.

Sick to his stomach, he had a sudden compulsion, a deep, sense of mission, to drive to the golf course. Villa said he wanted to play golf. It was his new hobby. The Tremboro golf course! He knew vaguely where it was. He released the parking brake and u-turned the auto back to the east. Why in the world was he going there and not to the police station? Why? Was he needed there?

The Mercury Golf Club sprawled just outside the city limits and was still open for business as though no military raid upon the city was in progress. As the riders trotted down Hole in One road, Venzula spotted some small groups of men playing golf in the distance, some in their funny golf hats, just like earlier in the morning. On an open patio to the left of the clubhouse, men in fashionable golf clothes sat eating lunch. Venzula smiled at their obliviousness. Their ignorance. The trio of soldados dismounted and tied off their horses' reins to a parking lot fence, beside other horses, coaches and autos.

A teenage boy, dressed in sporty clothes ran from the side of the building.

"Shall I take charge of the horses?" he said, in almost a British accent. "Oh, sir, you are back again."

"Si, we are back, but oh no. No," Venzula said in a sing-song pattern. "We are only here for a few minutes. Leave them here. Gracias."

The boy ran off.

"He is a nice boy," Venzula said. "He is from California, here with the beautiful manager."

Venzula had only formally met with the manager that morning. He has salivated over her from afar the night before. Miss April March, the female golf pro from Palm Springs, California. April was pleased with the celebrity visit of Pancho Villa and had several posed photos taken of the visit. Venzula planned on finding Miss March, and forcefully asking her for several "gifts" if need be, one of which was the bag of clubs that Villa used that morning. She should be honored, he will tell her. If the manager refused? Then a violent robbery would occur, stealing much more than the clubs.

What was Venzula's own personal quest? He also had a habit of at least one rape in each city, village or fort they conquered. Who shall it be here? Who? And a memory of this US raid will be made for all to fear the great Generalissimo Pancho Villa and his army. Who knows, perhaps next, perhaps someday, the Villa army would take back these parts of Texas for Mexico, as they fulfill the great "Plan of San Diego."

Then they heard a women yelling and screaming from inside the golf club. They looked at each other curiously. The three men walked up the sidewalk, through the revolving doors and into the stylish golf clubhouse. Once inside, the disturbance was apparent.

Celesta the bald witch was standing before the glass counter screaming in broken English and Spanish. Two men, one old, one young, listened to her with impatient faces. The manager, April March stepped out of an office to witness the commotion.

"Muy buenito, huh?" Venzula whispered to, and elbowed the man in the maroon sombrero. But the man remained expressionless.

"What is going on?" April asked the counter clerks, "can I help someone?"

"Dis woman, Senora March, she wishes to have a golf club that Pancho Villa used this morning."

"A...club?" April March said.

"Yes! I need dis club," the witch said. "Do you people not know what is going on in de city? Villa and his men are raiding Tremboro right now. Dey will steal everything! I must stop him!"

"With a golf club?" the employee asked.

"I must..." but Celesta was interrupted.

"Please, please," Venzula said, stepping forward. "Please let me help."

Celesta saw them, turned to him and backed away, crouched and ready for trouble.

"I am here to get des clubs also, but as a gift to my general." He turned to April. "Dis woman is of course insane, huh? A witch! Pero, Generalissimo Villa had such a happy time here dis morning that just an hour ago, before he left for Mexico - and she is lying about such a raid of your city - he asked me, he said, 'I wonder if...I wonder if de, de golf club-house would present to me, the wonderful bag of golf clubs that I used?' He would be forever greatful."

Miss April March leaned an arm on the counter and thought about it.

"Enrique," she said, "can you find that bag of clubs from this morning?"

"Si, Miss March."

"Good."

"Ooooh dis...dis is wonderful. Wonderful. Now. Now as to the matter of dey witch here. What sort of black magic would she use with one golf club? Hmmmm. I wonder, I wonder if we could step inside your office for just one moment and we will solve dis problem."

April March stared at him. She looked at the witch. The witch slowly shook her head no again.

"Please..." Venzula said, stepping toward her office to nudge her in.

"Please. Arturo, could you escort dis witch in too?"

Arturo grabbed the witch's elbow.

"Javier, would you please get the bag when Enrique returns?" Venzula said to the man in maroon sombrero.

"Ah, si, Colonel."

April March suspiciously headed for the office with Venzula, Arturo and the witch followed. They walked in single file. Arturo shut the door behind them. April rounded her desk to sit down, but Venzula grabbed her arm before she could, and pulled his pistol. He put the pistol barrel under her neck.

"No noise," Venzula said.

"No noise," Arturo repeated, pressing his knife tip onto the witch's rib.

April March gasped. Celesta sneered.

Venzula tore off April's clothes, ripped her stockings and raped her on the desk. The office was not large and their feet repeatedly hit the witch's and Arturo's thighs. She remained quiet. When he was done, he wiped his mouth and grinned.

"If you scream?" Venzula said. "I will kill everyone in the lobby. Dey golfers too. And I will kill you. You will stay in dis office for an hour, as I might have a beer in the bar before we leave, you know? A good Mexican beer. You do not want everyone here dead."

He straightened his clothes. Put on his hat and he, and Arturo with the witch in tow, left the office for the lobby.

The two workers stood behind the counter. Javier had the golf bag of clubs slug over his shoulder, the tops of the clubs shoving his maroon sombrero down over his brow.

"Thank you, Miss March," Venzula said with a smile, back into the office and he shut the door.

"And thank you gentlemen," Venzula said to the workers.

The three man and the witch left through the front doors.

Venzula stopped on the front sidewalk. He looked to the left, to the Hole 1 tee-off area and a maintenance building beside it. Then he looked at the witch. He looked her up and down.

"You know?" we are not finished here yet," Venzula said.

He grabbed the witch's other arm and led the small group across the tee-off box for that building.

"Let er' go," Gunther said sternly.

The men stopped, turned and stared at Johann Gunther standing about 15 feet away. The bald witch yanked free from their hand grips and stumbled over to the side of the building.

Venzula stood in the middle, his now free hand posed, still up in the air from where the witch escaped. He did not smile, nor frown. To Venzula's left, the man with the maroon sombrero stood, and he frowned. Deeply. With fear. His eyes were wide and he dropped the golf bag from his shoulder. It fell over. The soldier to the right lowered his head. This man knew to take one step away from Venzula. Then another. Gunther saw this, and he knew instinctively that with each little side step he was more outflanked and the distance between the men increased making them harder to shoot.

Instantly, Gunther drew his brace of pistols. He stepped off to his right and fired four times into Venzula with his left-handed gun, to his chest and stomach. Venzula, surprised at this abrupt quickness, surprised that his outflank trap had not yet set, tried to reach for his pistol but, as the bullets pounded into his torso, he couldn't grasp his pistol well and as he fell, the gun fell to the putting green grass.

Gunther shot the man to the right. His walking sideways had the soldado's body in an awkward position to draw. His face disappeared, disfigured in an explosion. He too was pulling his pistol when Gunther's two rounds hit him in the head and shoulder. Dead man standing, he collapsed.

Gunther's head snapped back to the man in the maroon sombrero. Since he was to be the third to shoot, that man had more time to do something. But, in that precious time, he did nothing. His hands flew so far up, his sombrero slipped off his head, over half his face.

The bald witch screamed in shock at first, then looked gleeful, then fell into a sadness. Golfers in the distance turned and watched in shock for a moment, then dropped to the grass or ran for cover.

Gunther stared at the remaining man, his left-hand re-volver still held two bullets, aimed at the man's head. He dropped the other gun in his right hand and pulled the Ger-man Luger from his shoulder holster. The man in the maroon sombrero spread his fingers out and, with his left hand pulled his pistola out with his thumb in the trigger guard like one would pick up a dead, stinking rat. He tossed the gun on the green.

"No senor," the man said. "No, no senor."

Gunther holstered the revolver and kept the Luger aimed

at him, belly high. He glanced at the two downed men to his right. Venzula was still gurgling about something. Gunther walked to him and stood over him. He took the sights of his Luger off of the man with maroon sombrero and aimed them at Venzula's face. Venzula's eyes opened wide. He tried to speak again, but couldn't.

"Hard to speak, aint it? My bullets cut through your lungs you piece of shit. Makes it…it…kinda' hard to speak."

Venzula made faces. Faces probably not meant to communicate. Just contractions of shock and pain.

Gunther nodded, leaned over a bit and said slowly…

"And today. Today, I saved all the horses."

He shot Venzula in the neck. His neck tore open in a wet slab of a mess.

He walked to the third man.

"Como se llama?" Gunther asked him when close, Luger aimed at his belly.

"Javier Fusetti."

"Comprende English?"

"Si, si senor, Y…yes."

"Javier, Javier, why don't you get on your horse over there…get on your horse and ride north. You don't need to be attached to all this. Get on…your horse …and just ride to Dallas. Or Oklahoma City. Go north. Just go north. There are Mexicans in all these places. They are happy. Working. Living their lives. With families. With none of…all this. Fuck this Revolution. It never ends, Javier. It ends if you make it end. Go and meet them up north. Live there. Meet a senorita. Have a family. Be happy. Sing songs at Christmas."

The man stuttered and shook.

"You don't have to be…attached to all this." Gunther waved his gun barrel in circles.

"Si…yes."

"Comprende?" Gunther said. "Understand."

"Si…yes.…yes." He put his hands down slowly.

Employees ran out the front door to see what had happened.

Gunther reached into his pocket and pulled out a $10 dollar bill from his gun money, pocket stash and handed it to him.

"Here ya go. Here's some US dollars to get you outta here."

He motioned with his gun over to the horses.

"Go. Go on. Geet'."

The man walked off.

"Best get yer hat! It's sunny in Texas too, Javier, and yer gun too, There's plenty of snakes on the way."

The man stopped, stooped and grabbed his maroon sombrero and pistola. Gunther watched him walk off and get on his horse.

He knew where north was and took off at a gallop while Gunther walked over to the witch. She was sitting on a park bench by the small building. He sat on the bench with her and flicked his hat back on his head.

"He's free at least," Gunther mumbled.

April March burst out the front doors wrapped in a big clubhouse towel, with shreds of her clothes sticking out of the top and bottom. Her face was bleeding. Her hair a mess. She had a short-barrelled, chrome revolver in her hand, held down at her side. She stopped to see the dead mess on the tee-off box.

"He killed dem," Celesta said.

"You killed them?" April March asked.

"Yes maam," Gunther said.

April March lifted the pistol barrel toward Venzula's body. With a most placid expression, she leaned way over and shot the corpse in the groin. The single blast rolled the nearby grass and carried across the grounds. Even Gunther winced a bit in surprise. Nearby employees and customers couldn't believe their eyes and ears.

The bald witch rested her elbows on her knees and wrapped her whole face in her hands for a few seconds.

"You...you are unhurt?" Celesta asked Gunther. "I heard about the gun store. You face a dozen of these villains without a scratch? You are unhurt?" she asked. "Dis is some kind of magic."

"I am unhurt, Celesta," Gunther said, loading his guns.

"Dis is some kind of magic," she repeated.

"Yeah. Some kinda' magic," he repeated quietly.

"Last night, you have become de shaman."

He looked at her curiously. He knew what a shaman was and how someone became one. He was just too exhausted to question her about it.

April March coughed and then gagged.

"You okay?" Gunther asked April.

"No," she said. "But better now." She pointed a thumb back at the corpses.

Gunther nodded. He eyed the woman and deduced what had happened to her. The same fate for Celesta had he not interrupted Venzula.

"Well, I am sorry it is so rowdy out here. You all...you got any coffee in there?" Gunther asked.

"Get this man some fresh coffee!" April shouted with a shrill voice. Her desk crew and waitresses were standing far back, afraid to get too close to the carnage.

"Black is fine," Gunther also shouted. He watched April walk back inside. he noticed she was barefoot, too.

"She was raped by Venzula."

Gunther nodded.

"I saw dis. I saw Jefe in town," the witch said.

"He okay?"

"Yes, he was riding your Black Magic horse."

"Where?"

"Some soldiers were trying to rob de bank, and when I left he was talking to dem."

"Hey, do the phones work out here?" he shouted to some employees who eventually crept forward, gawking back and forth at the bodies.

"Yes, sir."

"Call the Marshal's Office and see where they need help, will ya?"

"Yes, sir."

Assorted golfers wandered up and gaped at the dead bodies, then sneak-peeked back and forth at Gunther, with the "*he* did this," looks.

"You men best get home," Gunther said. "Villa started raiding the city and you'd best get home or get to your businesses. Give yer daughters some guns. I've already rescued one."

They all looked at each and some left for the clubhouse. Some remained.

"The boys? Dey are...dead?" the witch asked.

He looked over at her. He shook his head in irony. How could she know?

"They are dead, Celesta."

"Madre of God. I knew this. I knew dis would happen to dem. I saw it. I saw it the moment you walked from de train station. I tried to stop you. I tried."

"Yes you did," Gunther said. "No magic for them, huh?"

"No. Only for you."

"Only for me. Why's that?"

"Because you have many deeds to perform, Johann Gunther."

"Deeds, huh?"

April March, sans the revolver, returned with the cup of coffee, her towel better tied and stuffed around her. And, she was now wearing shoes.

"Thank you, maam."

"You say you don't play golf, Mr Gunther?" she asked, while he sipped the hot brew.

"Noooo. Not yet."

"If you ever come for another visit, consider yourself a Guest of Honor here."

"Well, I will." Gunther stood, reached into his back pocket, pulled out his wallet and handed her a business card.

"I have a little company called Remedies back home. We...solve people's problems."

"I'll bet you do," she said, looking at the card.

"Call me if you ever need any help."

"Any...remedies, I sometimes need remedies." She turned to talk to her customers that had lingered. Her voice sounded more gracious.

An employee appeared at the front and shouted, "The Marshal's Office said the soldiers have left. They said to tell you that your friends are fine."

Gunther about collapsed back on the bench, almost spilling his coffee.

"You need some of this?" he asked Celesta.

She nodded and took the cup for a sip.

"No more deeds," he said to the bald witch.

"Si. No more deeds *here*. But dere are deeds of life. Like...like to keel Villa. To keel Pancho Villa."

"He's long gone to Mexico, Celesta. Across the Rio Grande. Back with his big army. I cannot attack an army."

"Not now, Johann Gunther. Not now. You will have your place. Your time. You are now de shaman. You have had your shaman night."

He looked at her again, curiously.

"Warlock," she said.

"I...ahhh, I'm no warlock, Celesta."

She just stared at his profile.

Gunther got the cup back and took another sip. He looked off to the south. Then he looked at the two remaining horses out front, standing, shifting their body weight and swinging their tails.

"Celesta, it looks to me like you now have two new horses," he said, pointing at them out on the lot.

"I have no use for de horse. I walk everywhere I need to go."

"I guess the golf course now has two new horses, then. Well, Miss Celesta, you may walk everywhere, but would you at least accompany me on a drive back to town?"

"Si. God bless you, Mr Gunther," she said.

"I didn't sneeze," he said.

Chapter 19: Caravan of Vagabonds

"Yesterday was a fire and brimstone day for the people of Tremboro, Texas. A few days ago we welcomed the arrival of General Pancho Villa and his Revolutionaries, a movement for the poor people of Mexico that the editorial staff of this newspaper openly support. After much fanfare and welcome, introductions and touring, yesterday Villa and his men attempted to isolate and raid our fair city, attacking its businesses and raping and murdering its people, as is often Villa's methods in Mexico.

But thanks to the Lord and the good work of our Marshal Preston Heston, himself wounded in the attacks, and his police force and his mastering of a posse of able-bodied, brave and armed Tremboro and Clant County citizens, this raid was nipped in the bud, else it could have been far, far worse.

Still, many of our fellow citizens have still been raped,

hurt and killed. We mourn the victims of these crimes. Mayor Williams said his goal is to support these victims and their families.

To our surprise, somehow, authorities in San Antonio were reached yesterday morning even after the phone and wire lines were cut and before the raids began. How this happened we do not know. Perhaps it was the work of our two, brave, murdered railroad linemen Larry Barone and Archie Christian. May they rest in peace. God help their families.

This warning saved the afternoon train from a derailment on the exploded rail lines and brought a team of law enforcement officers by automobile and horseback into Tremboro early last evening. By then, Marshal Heston and his men were wrapping up their small war against the Revolutionaries.

The Governor of Texas himself, has been made aware of these events and a task force from San Antonio is also in route to report, investigate, and repair the railroad, phone and telegraph lines.

Order will be restored in our fair city. Say a prayer tonight for Tremboro, for Marshal Heston, and all the people we lost, all the people hurt, and all the people who risked their lives to save her."

- Editor in Chief, The Tremboro Endeavor

****

While the morning papers were delivered across the city to news-hungry citizens, some men were busy on the front parking lot of Cravios Casa Funeraria. Gunther was one. He checked the saddle on Black Magic. The horse remained calm near the running engine of the mining company truck that manager Delarosa offered up to get the small troop back to San Antonio. They could not wait days for the rail lines to be fixed, for the two coffins in the bed of the truck must be delivered to the family in Brownsville as soon as possible.

Jefe sat on the open bed between the coffins with a hand on each one, his feet dangling off the end of the truck. He wasn't fully crying, but he had to dab his eyes with a hankerchief. They needed to get back to civilization just to phone the Whittle family and inform them of the disgusting, horrible news of Josh and Whistler's demise.

Calabash was busy on the bed of the open truck, helping the Cravios brothers cinch the coffins in place.

Bullwhip Pierce was already on a horse he'd just bought on the New Mexico budget. He sat on the mount like a stocky monument, his ever-present whip wrapped around the horseshoe on his gun belt.

"He alright?" Bullwhip leaned over and asked Gunther about Jefe.

"As good as can be expected," Gunther said. "He's a father. A really good father, and he's got little boys and girls back home. He loves kids. He really took to those two boys."

Bullwhip nodded. He watched Jefe for a bit, then rode over to him. Jefe glanced up, and they just looked at each other. Bullwhip reached out his hand and Jefe took it. They talked, then...

"Heavenly Father..." and Bullwhip whispered a prayer with a lowered head.

Gunther watched the Muslim and the Baptist pray for the boys. For life? For good? Whatever was. Whatever's left. Jefe, the valiant soldier, the impeccable scout and war vet, did then openly cry.

Rock Candy Randy walked up to the funeral home with his odd gait, in a suit too big for him, carrying two suitcases. Hotel owner Renkowitz walked beside him with another suitcase.

"Nister Nunther," Randy said when he got close.

"Good morning, Randy," Gunther said and nodded to him.

Randy and Renkowitz put the suitcases in the bed of the truck. Calabash got them and carried them to front of the bed. Then he returned and offered a hand up to Randy.

"Here we go there, young fella'," Calabash said, and Randy climbed into the truck.

"We'll take good care of him," Gunther said to Renkowitz.

"I know you will," Renkowitz said. "And the missus and I will surely miss him. He was no trouble at all."

"Well...Gunther said, "we'll either put em' in a special school in Fort Worth, or...and I have a good feeling about this...or...let him stay with the Whittles in Brownsville. I know the family, and after all this...after all this I think they will take good care of him. Adopt him as their own. They'll get him the proper schooling he needs in Brownsville."

"I sure hope so, Gunth," Renkowitz said. "The boy needs a momma and daddy."

Gunther nodded.

They shook hands.

"Thank you for everything you've done here, Gunther."

"Do me a favor? Might outta thank Jefe too," Gunther said. "He's done a lot more than I did. And he ain't faring so well at the moment."

"Of course," Renkowitz said, looking over at Jefe. "I will," he said.

Renkowitz stepped over to Jefe and they exchanged some words.

Three horsemen approached from the east, Marshal Heston and two deputies.

"Y'all are off?" Heston said as he dismounted carefully with his arm and shoulder buried in a cast all the way up to his neck, but he still managed the smooth descent of a true horseman.

"Yes sir, we are," Gunther said. He waved his hand at the coffins. "We...we can't wait here. We gotta go."

"I understand. I understand. I wanted to thank you men for helping us. Without you figuring out what was gonna happen, we'd been in a helluva' pickle."

Bullwhip rode over to them.

"Bullwhip," Heston nodded to him, now aware the big

man was New Mexico law enforcement. "I don't guess I'll see you again, you being from New Mex."

"Oh, I am a Texan, sir. If they get a new governor here, I might return to the Texas Rangers. I can't abide by this governor. If so, ANY...time you need me. Just call the San Antone Ranger company. They'll get me in New Mex or if'n I'm back here in God's country."

Heston sighed, shook his head and said, "not much to say for God's country around here."

"Ohh, Marshal. it's all God's country and God's work. For whatever the reason," Bullwhip said.

Heston walked over to Jefe, reached up and shook his hand. And then he waved at Calabash sitting on the bed too. Jefe finally smiled.

"If y'all ever here again, ya' gotta stop by the police station. I couldna' done it without any of ya."

"Will do," Gunther said.

"God bless!" Bullwhip said.

"Hey, how's Miss April March doing?" Gunther asked.

"She'll be alright. She's tougher then she lets on. Ya know, she's from Detroit, and that ain't her real name. She's one tough lady."

Heston got back on his horse rather smoothly despite his wounds. He looked at the coffins again and shook his head.

"I don't envy ya, Gunth," Heston said.

The three lawmen tipped their Stetsons, turned their steeds and rode off.

The ambulance drove up. The two medics smiled broadly at Gunther. He waved back.

"What cha' gonna do with them?" Bullwhip asked.

"I promised them a job up north. Introduce them to some San Antonio doctors. They'll get some work somewhere. They are combat, vet medical people."

"You just a real Tex-Mex, Noah's Ark, ain't cha?"

"U.S., India, Afghanistan...China...yeah, if you only knew," Gunther said with a smirk, then threw a leg over his horse.

"Senors, you are ready to go," a Cravios brother said, leaping down from the truck.

"Muchas gracias, amigo," Gunther said as he climbed aboard Black Magic. "Thank you for all your help. The boys. they look...fine."

"Ready?" he asked the driver of the truck.

"Ready," Gunther said.

Jefe slid off the bed and climbed into the passenger seat in the cab of the truck.

Calabash rested on a steamer full of confiscated Mexican guns on the front of the bed, just behind the cab. Chueng gave them all the guns confiscated from the soldiers, for free.

"Vamanos, amigos," Gunther said.

A paper skeleton rippled past them in the wind on the street.

Bullwhip saw it. "The Day of the Dead is over," he said.

"Noooot quite," Gunther said, as Celesta appeared from across the street and ran up to Gunther.

"Here," she said, and hooked a string of beads on his saddle horn.

"You can touch dese one!" she said. "Dis is for your safe passage, and your meession."

"Mission?"

"Villa," she growled with disgust.

Gunther grunted and his unspurred boot tapped Black Magic into a walk.

"Bye, Celesta," Gunther said.

"Adios...warlock," she said.

Bullwhip looked over the two vehicles and the mix of people.

The truck started and rolled forward a bit.

"Hey," the driver said leaning out of the side window, "we'll beat ya to San Antoine."

"I know you will. But I'm not leaving here without my beloved new horse," Gunther said. "So go on ahead. Jefe knows where to go."

"Okay."

In minutes, the truck pulled quite a bit ahead.

"They'll probably have six flats on the way," Bullwhip said.

And for the first time in days, they both laughed.

Chapter 20: Mr. President, General Pershing is Here to See You

March 1923, Washington DC

To: General Pershing, United States Army
From: George Hall, Her Majesty's Service, Great Britain
Date: March 31, 1923

Dear General, it is both and honor and a pleasure to correspond with you, as I have heard much of your record. You have enquired through our governments, of my contacts with one Johann Gunther in Tremboro, Texas in 1916, events, leading up to and including what some call, the "Battle of Tremboro." No doubt, somehow through your extensive connections, you have discovered that Mr Gunther assisted me in Tremboro by filing some intelligence reports with my embassy in Washington DC, on the movements of the now deceased Pancho Villa.

First, Sir, allow me to brief you on my relationship with Mr Gunther. I was attached to the Diplomatic Corp in 1906, in northern Afghanistan, on the north side of what many refer to in general as the Khyber Pass. In summary, the area was seized and run by a renegade US Army Colonel Latissimo and various Russian counterparts. Their mission was to conquer the country in now what we call "The Great Game," and as an aside, collect any spoils they might amass for reward. Mr Gunther arrived with the British Military and saved the day in the most bloody of battles. In that time, Mr Gunther showed exceptional inspiration and heroism. He was almost killed, and I saw to it that he subsequently received the upmost treatment for his wounds in a British hospital in India, whereupon our relationship developed during that time.

In 1915, I was dispatched to Mexico on an undercover intelligence mission, to spy on Pancho Villa. When I saw Mr Gunther in Tremboro I was elated but concerned he might blurt out my name! But he did nothing of the sort. He is a man above reproach and ever an ally of good. I asked him for help, and that he did. He transported several of my dossiers, to include a summary of his own, to help my nation and yours as well, versus the impending World War.

I only saw him at a group dinner, and in passing later that night when I made a drop of the secret dossier to him. The next day, Pancho Villa decided to raid this town, in his accustomed devastating fashion. Villa wished to leave Tremboro before the raid, but first we played golf, and then we went to an automobile dealership, he, myself and several of his men. In short, Villa killed the store owner and stole two cars. We left in those cars for Mexico before the marauding began. To this day I regret my undercover role in this affair and my ability, or lack thereof, to interfere with Villa's many crimes. But, I was on an international mission of great import and was chained to my assignment. I do hope you understand my position.

In later years, we have asked for Mr Gunther's advice and even help in some affairs of Great Britain, in which he offered sterling service to us. Some of this help you are, no doubt, already aware.

You asked in your enquiry about my knowledge on the question, "Would Mr Gunther assassinate or participate in

*an assassination of Pancho Villa?" I have no evidence, nor
any knowledge of such an event.*

*As to your second question, neither myself nor the British
Secret Service believe that Mexican National Jesus Salas
Barraza, the man the Mexican government claims, is the sole
assassin of Pancho Villa. We believe Barrarza may have
taken some physical part in the assassination team. He may
well have paid some officials to be far from that crime, but we
believe, based on our sources, he is not the killer.*

God bless you, and Godspeed,
George Hall

December 1924, Washington DC

Snow in the early evening.

Snow on and around the White House grounds.

President Calvin Coolidge stood before the Oval Office
windows, watching it all fall down around him. He'd been
president for two months after Warren G. Harding suddenly
died of a heart attack. Much more than snow was falling
heavily upon him.

"Mr. President," a voice said softly from the open office
door. "Mr. President, General Pershing is here."

Coolidge turned, nodded and within a few seconds General Pershing and an aide entered, hats in hands, both their
Class A uniform jacket tops covered with snow.

"Have a seat. Have a seat."

"Thank you. This is Lt. Milligan Hawes, Mr President,"
Pershing said. "He's been with me throughout this investigation."

They all shook hands.

The soldiers slipped out of their winter jackets and laid
them across a chair by the door.

They sat on the two couches in the center of the room,
Coolidge on one, Pershing and Hawes on the other.

"Good to see you again, sir," Pershing said.

"It's a little different this time. I...am...in charge."

"I can only imagine, sir."

"A lot has fallen on my shoulders. We vice-presidents are not always informed of what is going on, here in this office. Where did you fellows come in from?"

"Texas. Train." Pershing said.

"Texas. That's a long trip."

"That is it, sir."

"I know President Harding had you on an investigation. I know little about it. Something to do with possible United States involvement with the assassination of Pancho Villa. I know that with your great familiarity and time down in Mexico, and having met Pancho Villa before, you were certainly the man to ask for help in this international matter. So, whatever have you learned about Villa's killing?"

"Well, sir," Pershing began. "President Harding was concerned that the United States might be linked to the assassination in some way. Any way. To begin with, on the day he died, Villa and his gang, his bodyguards, were in route to a nearby city in their cars. They were barricaded at a narrow intersection. There, they were ambushed and killed by a ragtag team, and indeed, as we had heard, we thought Johann Gunther was one of the killers."

"I see."

"Gunther was prior Army. Prior West Point. An officer under Roosevelt in Cuba, and years later did go hunting with, and did assignments for, President Roosevelt on occasion. So, some public recalcitrants can claim that Gunther has worked for the US Government. Even this...very office."

"So, was it true then?" Coolidge said.

"A witness said that in Villa's last words...he said something like, 'Johann? You?' You too?' Words to that effect, sir."

"Like Julius Caesar," Coolidge said. "This witness a good one?"

"We don't know, sir. He could not, or perhaps would not, pick Gunther's photograph out as one of the killers."

"I see."

"He may have been afraid, sir," Lt. Hawes spoke up. "The Mexican government has closed the case and any new witness or new testimony could be blamed for re-opening it. Spreading rumors. Doubts."

"And is it possible Villa knew Gunther on sight? Villa had met Gunther before, sufficient to recognize him like that? In that moment?"

"Yes, he did, sir. Their paths crossed a few times. Sometimes very briefly on mining business, as Gunther was hired to escort mining officials into Mexico. But, first in Tremboro, Texas. The center point of our investigation. Gunther thwarted what could have been a pillaging much like the Villa raid on Columbus, New Mexico."

"Thwarted?"

"Yes, sir. Gunther figured out what was going to happen, and ambushed the ambush, in so many words."

"Johann Gunther," Coolidge said in a breathy sigh. "Can this come back to haunt us? Good God. He's been attached to the White House."

"Yes sir. He was, but years ago." Pershing sat forward, leaning inward to the President. "I am not sure you know this sir, but, back when Roosevelt was lost on the Amazon in South America, presumably on one of his adventure trips?"

"Yes?"

"He wasn't lost, sir. When exploring, he was kidnapped by a Brazilian jungle gang."

"My God, I did not know that!"

"Almost no one does. They held him for ransom. President Wilson didn't know what to do at the time. Teddy's daughter has a...certain fondness for Gunther...she stepped in and got Gunther to rescue Teddy."

"Rescue him? Out of the Amazon jungle?"

"Yes, sir. He used...hot air balloons to travel. He and his team traversed over the jungle in balloons."

The President shook his head. "Unbelievable. Is there anything else he's done?"

"Yes. For one thing, we believe that Gunther was somehow involved with the Zimmerman telegraph from Germany to Mexico ."

"The Zimmerman...?"

"Yes, sir, a secret message sent from Germany to Mexico. I realize you are new to this office. In the Great War, Germany tried to conspire with Mexico to tie up our country with a small war over here, keeping us out of the World War over there. Gunther knew - from a Roosevelt-initiated mission in Afghanistan - a member of the British Intelligence. Since Gunther is German and speaks German, the Brits asked him to do something in 1917 involving the Zimmerman message. We do not know exactly what that was. The Brits won't tell us. But he performed some...service for Great Britain."

"For the greater good?"

"Yes, sir. Of course. It aided England. And therefore us too."

"Did you question Gunther?"

"About the Zimmerman message? No, sir. About Villa? Yes, sir. We questioned him last. After all the information was collected," the general said.

"What did he say?"

"Mr. President, we met him in Fort Worth at his lawyer's office. Downtown, Fort Worth. We first contacted Gunther by personal messenger at his detective office. Our messenger, a sergeant, insisted on waiting, as per ordered by me, for Gunther's reply. The short, scribbled, handwritten letter Gunther gave him delivered in reply had a Fort Worth phone number. When we called it, we learned it was the number of a lawyer for future reference."

"Did you tell him in your message exactly why you wanted to see him?" the President asked.

"I told him that we had questions about any involvement he may have had with Pancho Villa."

"Just that?"

"Just that. The next day, I received a phone call from the law office of Roberto Lopez. He is one of the best lawyers in the southwest, I am told. They agreed to met us, at Lopez's office three days later at 9 a.m."

"You went. How did that go? What did Gunther say?"

"Well, sir....."

Chapter 21: The Lost Gospel of Johann Gunther
November 1924, Fort Worth, Texas

Gunther, wearing a dark brown suit, white shirt and bolo tie sat at the large table in Roberto Lopez's conference room, a cup of black coffee inches from his fingertips. The clock on the wall struck and chimed nine times. On the eighth ring, the front door opened and in walked General Black Jack Pershing, in full uniform with two young lieutenants. Lopez's secretary led the team down the hall to the conference room.

Counselor Roberto Lopez was already standing. Gunther stood wearing a smile on his face, he stepped around the table and shook Pershing's hand, "General, I'm very proud to meet you, sir," Gunther said with affection.

"Thank you, Mr Gunther."

"I followed your work in Europe in the Great War. It must have been horrible."

"It was...horrible."

"Please sit down," Lopez said, shaking their hands. "Rob Lopez."

Gunther reached over and shook hands with the two officers. The duo sat, opened their briefcases and placed pads and pencils on the table. The secretary asked them if they wanted something to drink.

"Coffee's pretty good," Gunther suggested.

"Black coffee, thank you," Pershing said.

The two young officers shook their head no.

Lopez took his steaming cup and sat beside Gunther.

"Ready?" Pershing asked the two.

"Ready, sir," one said.

And one of the officers read from his pad, "December 3rd, 1924. Office of Roberto Lopez." He named the address and the parties present in the room. "You are Johann Gunther, born in Germany. Family immigrated in the 1880s through New York City. You joined the Army. Cavalry. Mustered out. Deputy marshal in Paris,Texas. Endorsed by the Governor of Oklahoma and Arkansas to attend West Point. Graduated. Saw action in Cuba and the Philippines. A mission in South Africa. China. A subsequent government mission in Afghanistan on record and others rumored but not on any official record. Now resides and works in Fort Worth, Texas, owner and operator of Remedies Investigations.

"You have done a few things for President Roosevelt, your superior in the Cuba engagement," Pershing added.

Pershing stared at Gunther waiting for an acknowledgment.

Gunther nodded.

Pershing waited.

Gunther waited.

"Through the years, it has been my...understanding...that you have had several meetings, or encounters with the infamous Pancho Villa of Mexico," Pershing asked.

Gunther waited.

Pershing waited, then continued.

"Our investigation..."

"Ah, excuse me," Lopez interrupted. "Did you say investigation?"

"Yes."

"This is an official government investigation?" Lopez asked.

"Well, yes."

"May I ask, is this a US Army investigation, in which

case my client has not been in the Army for a very long time."

"It is not," the General said.

"Yet, you are here representing the Army?"

"This is not a military investigation."

"Is it a police investigation?"

Pershing kind of grimaced.

"Because there are no representatives of law enforcement here at any level."

"No, let's just call it a...a...government investigation."

"And can you define that for us?"

"You have had several encounters with Pancho..." Pershing turned back to Gunther and tried to continue.

"Excuse me, General. You did not answer my question. I am afraid we cannot continue until we establish what sort of an investigation this is," Lopez said.

"Actually Mr. Lopez, this is more like an inquiry."

"From whom? Over what?"

"An inquiry from the President of the United States. Over how many times your client has met Pancho Villa."

Gunther sipped his coffee.

"The president?" Lopez said acting astonished.

"Yes. We are trying to tie up some past business... history... with Pancho Villa, as friend and foe to the United States. Mr Gunther can fill in some of these blanks."

He turned back to Gunther.

"Our records indicate that you have met or been in the same city...area...as Pancho Villa several times. The first was that unfortunate mess in Tremboro, Texas. Once again in El Paso area during the Revolution. And you have worked for several American mining companies as an escort and guide. Is this correct?"

"Are there any laws violated with any of this?" Lopez interrupted again.

"You're the lawyer, Mr. Lopez, is there?" Pershing sipped his coffee. "Are there any you can think of?"

"The international laws regulating business and business

contacts are difficult, and changing all the time. They are especially loose concerning Mexico. My client might have inadvertently not crossed all the T's and dotted all the I's in his older dealings with clients and the mining business, within very complicated and changing..."

"How about the crime of murder?" Pershing said, getting right to the point.

Gunther sat perfectly still.

"Murder!" Lopez declared.

"Have you ever met, or do you know a Jesus Salas Barraza?" Pershing asked.

Again, no answer. Just a Gunther poker face.

"Were you involved with, or anywhere near, or have anything to do with the assassination of Pancho Villa?"

"Don't answer that!" Lopez said. Lopez touched Gunther's shoulder and stood to say, "Murder, sir! That is for sure a crime, and though I am sure that my respected client, a man with endorsements from Theodore Roosevelt and several governors of Texas and Oklahoma to name only a few, and a Spanish war veteran, would have no such involvement in that, and even if he did? I will stop this witch hunt right now, and order my client to remain silent as is his right under the Constitution."

Lopez sat down. They all sat in silence. The only noise was the two tips of soft lead pencils scratching on paper.

"I have a witness who was there, and stated that the last words of Pancho Villa were 'and you too, Johann?'"

"How Shakesperean," Gunther said.

"How," Pershing replied.

"That is what Shakespeare said, Caesar said. Not even Plutarch could quote the last words of Caesar," Gunther said.

"Can you?" Pershing said. Pershing drummed his fingers on the table. "Can you quote the last words of Pancho Villa?"

No answer from Gunther.

Roberto Lopez made a displeased face at the continued questions.

"Hmmmm?" Pershing hummed.

Pershing stared at the floor for half a moment. He knew this interview was over, thanks to the protests of Lopez. But investigative protocol must be followed, and he had to try and ask.

Pershing said quietly, "To educate, train and inspire the corps of cadets..."

"...So that each graduate is a commissioned leader of character," Gunther finished the classic West Point quote.

They looked at each other. Both had to study Plutarch at West Point as well as know that motto, among so many such mottos.

"Have we not met somewhere before?" Pershing asked Gunther.

"No, sir. Close in the Philippines, but no."

"That was quite a mess they put us in, wasn't it?" Pershing said.

"Yes, it was. A muddy mess. I was glad to leave."

"Me too."

"Is that where you met your friend? This Jefe fellow? Cocoy?"

"Yes, sir, he fought with our side. Obviously. He mostly wanted his country to have a Western education system at the time. But, he returned here with me. We decided in Manila to open a detective agency."

"He seems like a good man. A good friend. A soldier. A scholar, from what our investigation gathered."

"Irreplaceable, sir. Overflowing with the best of character."

"And I presume, Mr. Lopez, that you are also Jefe's attorney?"

"That I am," Lopez said.

"Hmmm. And he too will be vigorously defended," Pershing said.

"Of course," Lopez said.

"I have learned a great deal about your's and Jefe's ordeal in Tremboro. From a Willin Calabash, and he..."

"Ha! How is he?" Gunther interrupted with a smile.

"He is fine."

"Where is he?"

"He's got a butcher shop in Nebraska."

"He was once a butcher. That...that makes sense, yes."

"...and from the others involved," Pershing finished his original thought. "You showed great leadership and improvisation in that situation. Rousing a city to its sudden defense. You could have just...ridden off. You could have armed up, sat your group in a hotel room and waited for them to pillage and then leave. They would have ignored you."

"I thought about both, sir," Gunther said.

"Way lesser men, lesser deeds have ben awarded great medals for what you did. To this day, the public doesn't really know what almost happened in Tremboro. On paper, sounds like a few feud murders and some cattle rustling. Car theft. Like some...rowdy Mexican soldiers committing some crimes. And no one down there really knows what you did to save the entire city," Pershing said.

"It did work out that way."

"Their history books claim that Marshal Preston Heston saved the day."

"That's fine with me. He did a lot. Did you speak to him too?"

"Heston was killed in a gunfight just a few years ago."

"Oh no. Oh hell. That's...that's bad...news."

Pershing finished his coffee.

"Seems like, the closer to Mexico you get, the better the coffee tastes," the general said.

Pershing stood and said, "Well, men, looks like we are done here."

The two officers looked a bit surprised, laid down their pencils and started packing up.

Lopez and Gunther also stood. Gunther rounded the table as they all exited the room. Gunther, side-by-side, walked with the General through the hallway.

"It was a pleasure to meet you, sir," Gunther said, "even under these circumstances. As I said, I have read about your

World War experience, as well as the expedition into Mexico. Perhaps we...we someday we might talk again."

They shook hands.

"Yes, under less *risky* circumstances. You have a private investigation business? Still?"

"Still."

"Well then perhaps I may hire you someday for something," Pershing said. "Take care of yourself, Mr Gunther."

Gunther took a few quick steps forward to shake the hands of the two young officers.

"West Point?" Gunther asked.

"Yes, sir."

"Yes, sir."

"You don't have to call me, sir. Those days are long gone. Good luck with your careers, men," Gunther said with an admiring smile.

The three men left the law office.

"That was really something," Lopez said.

From a window, with a curtain pulled aside, Gunther watched the men get into a car parked on the street.

"Yes, it was. You did an excellent job, Roberto."

"You said nothing incriminating," Lopez said.

"This ain't my first rodeo," Gunther whispered, watching the car drive off.

"Imagine them thinking *you* killed Pancho Villa!" Lopez said.

"Imagine that."

"Preposterous," Lopez said.

"PREEE-posteorus," Gunther said in a sigh.

Chapter 22: The Sins of Villa, The Sons of Whittles
December 1924, Washington DC

"Did he sign a witness statement?" the President asked.

"No sir, he did not."

"He refused?"

"We did not create enough of a statement *to* sign, sir."

"No..."

"No statement. He didn't answer any important questions on the advice of his attorney."

"Can we...close this out?"

"Nowhere else to turn, sir. And Mexico seems to have their lone suspect. A Jesus Salas Barraza has confessed shortly after the assassination, but many believe he was paid off to do so. In any case, he did not act alone. He was sentenced to a mere 6 months in jail and was...pardoned. Very unusual, especially for Mexico. Then, there was some local vaquero, an administrator of a neighbor's ranch owed Villa money. Some say he organized it. Some say, their local governor was involved. Then there are those who claim the federal government wanted to be rid of future troublemakers and future revolutions. Gunther may have worked with any of them. Or none. Or...all! Mexican murder, money, politics."

"Can anyone connect the Villa assassination to Wilson or Harding? Or…me?"

"No, sir. If Gunther participated…if...Gunther acted on his own to help in a plot? No. I, sir, if I might suggest, we should end this here. You are a new President, and are not responsible for the past. And no one knows that an American was even at the assassination. The whole thing is surrounded in rumors. Harding is dead. Just a few Mexicans have been named. A handful. And that handful exists in a twisted landscape of lies and fear. It seems no one else really...cares."

"It's murder, though."

"It's a murder in Mexico and no one really cares. Or they are afraid to care."

"I see."

"And we shouldn't care either," Pershing said.

"I see."

"If we push it? We are only pushing to open up more trouble."

"It won't come back on us?"

"It shouldn't."

President Coolidge nodded. He stood.

Pershing and Hawes stood and gathered up their coats.

"Where is Gunther now?" Coolidge asked.

"In Fort Worth. At his Remedies Detective Agency. He's older and bit gray, sir. He's longer in the tooth, as we say in the Army."

"And he can keep a few secrets?"

"Ohhh, yes. Gunther, I am told...he holds many secrets. Big secrets. This will only be one of many. If there is even a secret to hold."

"Let's hope so, General."

Coolidge nodded. "Thank you." He also nodded and winked at Lt. Hawes.

"Stay warm sir," Pershing said.

"And to you men, the same."

The cold night wind and snow hit them at the White House front door as Pershing and Hawes carefully walked down the steps, leary of possible ice under the white blanket. An Amy sedan waited outside on the driveway for them.

"I guess we'll never know if, or why Gunther was there to kill Villa," Hawes said as they descended the stairs like beginning, ice skaters.

"I guess not. Not exactly. The prosecutorial mind needs motive!" Pershing said. "There's revenge. Motive. But we need more than that."

An aide opened the back car door, and the men climbed in. Another aide in the front seat handed Pershing a few files.

"Good visit, sir?" the aide asked.

"Good enough, Corporal."

The car started down the White House drive to Pennsylvania Avenue. Pershing shuffled though the files, spotted one and then opened it eagerly. He read the one-parchment page report inside. With raised eyebrows, he handed the report to Hawes.

Hawes read it and turned wide-eyed to the general.

"Last week I asked about this," Pershing said. "A whim. The Whittle name was familiar to me for some reason and I waited until we got back to DC and asked headquarters to look it up. Lt. Lancy Whittle was killed in the battle of Juarez. He was an observer and hit by a Mexican mortar. And a Sgt. Walter Whittle, of the 13th Cavalry Regiment was killed in Villa's raid at Columbus, New Mexico, in 1916. Villa himself was there, witnesses claim. My expedition to hunt Villa started over that very raid, and Walter Whittle was listed as a casualty in the reports. I somehow remembered that last name. I knew that name. Now I know."

"Sons of..." Hawes mumbled quietly.

"Sons of. Yes. So, four...*four* of four of the Whittle sons were killed by Pancho Villa," Hawes said.

"More or less, yes. By the actions of Pancho Villa. Not by Villa's hands himself, but..." Pershing said.

"But..." Hawes said, "by Villa."

"But *because* of Pancho Villa," Pershing finished. "That might be even more of a motive for Gunther?"

"We...well...this...we have to tell..."

"Speculation. It's over, Lieutenant," Pershing said, closing the folder. He stared out the window into the frigid night.

"I hunted all over Northern Mexico for Pancho Villa. I had orders from the president then to kill him. If Gunther did help kill him years later? He just finished my job."

"Francisco "Pancho" Villa (born José Doroteo Arango Arámbula; June 5, 1878–July 20, 1923) was a Mexican revolutionary leader who advocated for the poor, education, peace, freedom and land reform. He helped lead the Mexican Revolution, which ended the reign of Porfirio Díaz and led to the creation of a new government in Mexico. Today, Villa is remembered as a folk hero, and a champion of freedom of the lower class people of Mexico." - History Biography

The Last Chapter 23: The Grudges of Johann Gunther

November 1924, Fort Worth, Texas

Gunther descended the brick stairs in the backyard of Roberto Lopez's law office. He'd just met one of the great generals in US history, but he had also just been accused of murder. It wasn't the first time. Probably wouldn't be the last.

The well-dressed, office janitor worked around the yard polishing some brass lamps.

"That was fast, Mr Gunther."

"It was very fast, Phillip."

"I hope things went your way. Your horse had a little water while waiting."

"Oh, good. Thanks," Gunther said, walking up to Black Magic.

"Not many clients ride up on a horse these days."

"Most drive up, huh?" Gunther asked.

"That they do."

"Well, it's such a nice day."

"That it is."

Phillip jumped quickly to untie the reins from a stone column. Gunther was about to mount the horse, but all this discussion of Tremboro caused him to stop and look at the barely noticeable, vertical scars on the horse's neck. After all these years, Black's hair still hadn't covered over the torture. Black turned to look at him. Gunther smiled.

"Howdy, Black," he whispered and patted the neck. He climbed on.

"Careful riding," Phillip said. "Those cars out there..."

"We will."

Gunther and Black Magic made it to the end of the brick driveway. To the right was the main avenue. Too many cars, some horse drawn carriages, but mostly autos and trucks. Horse people of the prosperous Fort Worth downtown area knew all the back streets and alleys to get around safely. They turned left, away from traffic. But, rather than return to the Remedies Detective Agency office, Gunther and Black Magic went north instead. North to a bluff overlooking the Trinity River.

Once there, Gunther dismounted, dropped reins and stood. Black Magic's head butted his shoulder, snorted and then looked for some November grass to eat. Gunther took off his suit jacket and threw it over the saddle.

The view of the river was not grand, not like some parts of the Rio Grande, but it was high and good enough for now. He saw a lot of North Tarrant County below. Recent rains still fed the Trinity. It looked like a mini-Mississippi. But despite the view, his mind wandered. All this concern about who killed Pancho Villa. He thought back to the last time he saw Mr. Whittle...

****

July 4th, 1921 Brownsville, Texas

The bedroom was large and somewhat dark, decorated with the heads of various hunted Texas animals. A nurse led Gunther across the room to stand before a large bed. In the bed under numerous blankets and yet still shivering, lay the pale, balding Wilhelm Whittle, in his 70s and covered also, inside, with some form of cancer. To the right of the bed in a simple wooden chair sat a concerned Rock Candy Randy, now in his 20s. The room stank of dying flesh and bed-ridden, bowel movements.

"Thank you for coming, Johann," Whittle said.

"You're welcome."

"Nello Nister Nunther," Randy said.

"Hello Randy."

"Please sit. Sit," Whittle said.

Gunther did.

Whittle crab-crawled back with great effort to sit up a bit higher in the bed.

"How are you? How have you been?" Whittle asked.

"I'm fine, Will, fine."

"How is Jefe?"

"He is more than fine. He doesn't act, think or move his age. He never changes."

"Oh that's good news. Are you still, are your still working? Do you still have Remedies?"

"I still do, Yes. We still provide some remedies for whomever we can. Yes."

"I am going to ask you to do something, Johann. Ah...a favor. But, it is a business deal too. I've asked you to come all

the wayhere and listen to it. Please. Please don't be angry
with me, when you hear it."

"Okay."

"Vera and I have had four sons. Randy here is like my
fifth. My fifth and adopted son, that you brought to me.
To...us." His eyes watered. "I ... we love him, as much as our
others."

Randy stared at the top blanket on the bed with his usual
half-smile. He rocked slowly, but the smile was a bit brighter
now with those words.

"Through the years, my boys, have tried and done great
things. Josh and Whistler, as you know, were taken so young.
And I remind you, sir, I remind you that I never blamed you
for what happened. I forced you to take them to Tremboro
against your stern advice. Jefe too. I damn well know who
was at fault. I know Jefe loved those boys too."

"He did," Gunther said and nodded.

"Every son I had has died at the hands of Pancho Villa.
None directly, not by his hand alone, but by the hands of
those around him. By his wishes, by his commands, his influ-
ence. His damn will be done. Villa is a criminal and a killer,
an uneducated hog. Now, he sits like an outlaw king out there
in Northern Mexico."

Gunther nodded again. Randy stared at the blanket.

"You told me once years ago, Johann, that you were...you
could be called upon to be a gunfighter. You told me that you
were *not* an assassin. Not a killer for hire. Not a regulator.
Not a hitman, the likes of these organized criminals. Instead
though...however, you have killed the likes of those bad men.
Like Gawdy Shirts, and so many more you never told me
about. You have killed Villa's henchmen."

Gunther squirmed just a bit in his seat. Where was this
going?

"I want you to kill Pancho Villa," Whittle said.

"Villa." Gunther repeated solemnly.

"Pancho Villa, for orchestrating each event that killed
each one of my and Vera's beautiful sons. And for killing the

sons and daughters of ALL the people he killed."

"I...I..." Gunther stuttered.

"I don't want you to fly to Northern Mexico and shoot him in the head with a hunting rifle. I don't expect that from you. I wouldn't ask you to do that."

"What then?"

"With some of these other men you killed, you carried a grudge against them, a grudge for who they were and what they'd done. I want you to carry a new grudge, Johann. The kind of grudge you carried for all these other killers and vicious men. When the time was right? When the time was right...you...remembered those grudges and took advantage of the...the situation."

Silence from Gunther.

"You get around. You have worked for presidents. You have worked for American businesses involved with Mexico. Miners. You still go to Mexico. I want you, if the time is ever ripe, to kill Villa."

"I do want to kill him," Gunther confessed. "For your sons and for all his crimes. All those people he killed. There is no jail, no justice appropriate for that skunk, som-bitch."

"I will pay you $8,000 if and when you do it. I will be dead soon. If I showed you my stomach right now, Johann, you...you would vomit."

Randy's eyes widened and he nodded his head in agreement.

"It will be etched in my private wishes. It will be explained to my private attorney, Rendell Quest. He's here in Brownsville. Nothing in writing. If and when you do this, if the opportunity arises, contact Rendell Quest. A bank draft for services rendered will be cut. He is a young man and he will outlive us both."

Gunther leaned forward in his chair and looked at the dying man and Randy, his adopted son. The last "son."He rolled his hat brim in his hands between his legs. Then he spoke.

"I will carry this grudge for you. Numerous people may

beat me to it. He steals cattle from his neighbors. He gambles and never pays his debts. The Mexican governments are always afraid he might rise up and challenge them. There are many blood revengers. Plots. If I hear of such things? If I can? I will help them. I will kill or help kill Pancho Villa."

"Good. Good. Vera has been dead for 3 years." His lips quivered. A single tear traveled down his right cheek. "She *despised* Villa. It would be some kind of magic for her to reach from the grave like this and get this done. I will be dead...soon, too. And...and I will still reach from my grave for this. It's...it is like magic."

"Like some kind of black magic," Gunther said in a growling whisper.

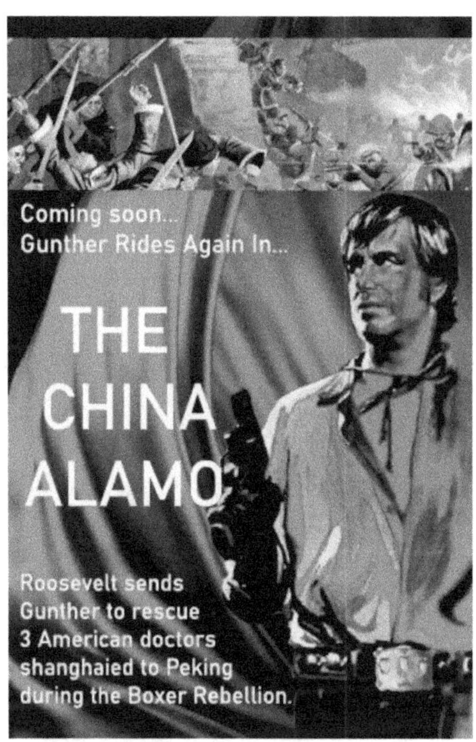

Coming soon...
Gunther Rides Again In...
THE
CHINA
ALAMO
Roosevelt sends
Gunther to rescue
3 American doctors
shanghaied to Peking
during the Boxer Rebellion.

Wolfpack Publishing presents...
BE
BAD
NOW
HOCK HOCHHEIM
BLOOD
RUST
HOCK HOCHHEIM
Two Police Crime-Fighting, Action, Adventure Thrillers

The State Department Should Give Columbus a Severe Reprimand for Being So Close to the Border

SANTA FE NEW MEXICAN

VILLA INVADES THE U.S.

BANDITS BURN AND KILL IN COLUMBUS

"DEATH TO AMERICANS" PANCHO'S CRY; WANTS TO CHOKE HATED GRINGO

AMERICAN TORN FROM WIFE'S ARMS, SHOT LIKE A DOG AND ROASTED

Colonel Slocum and Thirteenth Cavalry

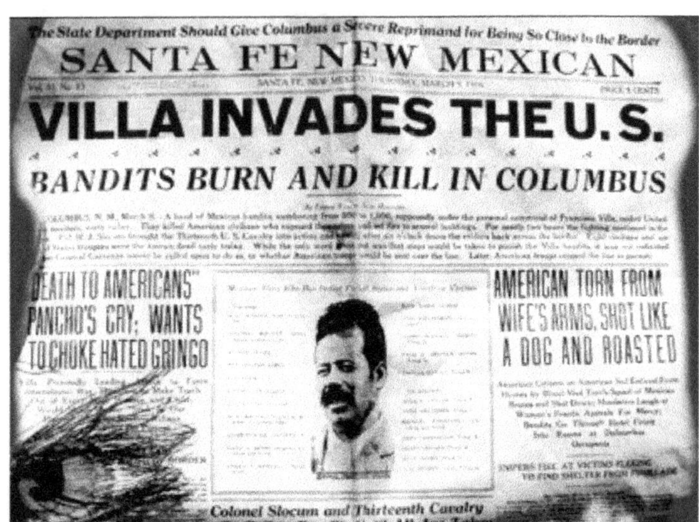

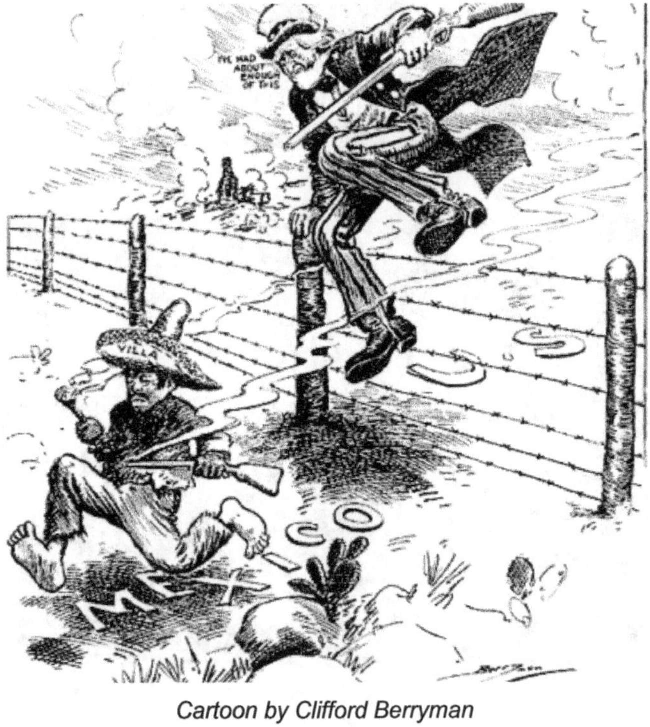

Cartoon by Clifford Berryman